A Christmas Wish

A Yuletide Creek Series

Kimberly Thomas

Chapter One

Suitcases overflowing with clothes. Empty bookshelves were already gathering dust in the abandoned office. No curtains by the windows.

No silver bells or boughs of holly.

That wasn't the way Melissa thought she'd be spending Christmas. But how could she expect anything better after all that had happened in the past several years?

Her eyes found the clock still sitting on the pastel walls in the living room every couple of seconds. Every time she thought she was done, she'd remember something else. And time was running out.

"Keys! Keys!" she mumbled to herself and started rummaging around in her purse. It wasn't there. "Kids! Has anyone seen my keys?" she shouted to Max and Gemma, who were still upstairs. Her heart started to race as she ran from one suitcase to the other.

"Mom!" Gemma screamed. Melissa heard the door bang upstairs shortly before what sounded like a stampede on the stairs, and a frantic Gemma hopped onto the landing and slid over to her. "I can't find my camera."

"Have you seen the car keys?" Melissa asked, completely ignoring her, as she turned about the room, reopening suitcases she'd barely closed earlier.

"No," Gemma replied with unconcern. "My camera."

Melissa stared at her in disbelief for a couple of seconds before she sighed. "There's nothing much left to check, honey. We've already packed up most of what we'll need for the trip. Are you sure it wasn't sent ahead with the other things?"

"I don't know," she wailed, her green eyes growing glossy as she stood with her shoulders sagging as she'd just lost the most important thing to her in the world. "Maybe. But I don't want to go, and then we don't have it."

"Gemma, it's just a camera. Even if we leave it, it's replaceable," Melissa replied and threw her hands in the air.

"Yeah," Max said as he bounded down the stairs looking his calmest. "Not like you ever use the thing."

"You shut your mouth!" Gemma said as she spun to face him, her green eyes flashing and her dark brown hair swishing against her shoulders from her ponytail. "What else am I going to do in the woods besides take pictures of birds?"

"Children!" Melissa cried and palmed her face. She sucked in a deep breath and smoothed her shoulder-length dark-brown hair backward. It was an exact match to Gemma's, while Max had dirty-blond hair that looked like Peter's— his dad.

But he was the last person Melissa wanted to be thinking about.

All she still needed was to get packed rather than

listen to her children fussing. "Can you both please just get the rest of your things together so we can go?"

"I don't even want to go," Gemma complained. "What's in Yuletide Creek anyway?"

"Family," Melissa told her. "And Aunt Elaine is looking forward to seeing us, so let's just go," she groaned.

"But why couldn't we just visit her for the holidays and come back here?" Gemma asked as her face fell.

"Because this isn't our home anymore," Melissa replied with a heavy heart. She sighed as her eyes swept the once-vibrant living space and remembered the many times her family had gathered there for family game night. Or movie night. Or had stayed up late the night before Christmas watching movies and drinking hot chocolate.

Now, it just felt empty. There were too many sad reminders of the once-happy marriage she'd had. But it had just been her. Peter had been a good husband for over a decade. They got married soon after Melissa had graduated high school. They'd made big plans for a life together — marriage, the house, car, kids, and the white picket fence. And it had seemed as if it was all coming together for a while. He was a stockbroker, and he seemed to love his job.

But as time waned, the children started growing up, and Max and Gemma were both in high school. Peter decided to call it quits.

That's right! He just gave up on the marriage. He switched careers to something he said was more exciting than his "dull domestic and corporate existence." His words had cut her to the core.

He picked up a job as a traveling salesman and moved south. Melissa thought he was just going through a phase, so she'd tried to be patient and give him some space. However, that small hole he made when he left quickly widened into a crack the size of the Grand Canyon when, a year later, she hadn't heard a word from him. When she filed for divorce, she got back the signed letter, but he made no demands about custody nor requested visitation.

He abandoned them. Without a single word or backward glance, he left her with all the shattered pieces and two extra broken hearts.

"I wish Dad was here. Then we wouldn't have to move!" Gemma exclaimed.

"But he isn't here, is he?" Melissa fired back. "Now go and get the rest of your things."

Their faces fell as they dragged themselves back up the stairs, widening that hole inside Melissa a little bit more.

But she couldn't worry about that. It was a six-hour drive to Yuletide Creek, and time was already against them. She couldn't get her head together, and then there were the keys.

"Where did I put them?" she asked as she ran into the kitchen. Sure enough, they were on the counter, and she sighed with relief just as her phone started ringing. "Not the best time," she said in a singsong voice as she pulled it from the pocket of her jeans.

"Mom! Hey," she answered and cradled the phone between her ear and shoulder as she tried to lock the suitcase all over again.

"It's almost Christmas. What are you doing this year?" she asked.

"Mom," Melissa groaned and stood. She wasn't particularly interested in answering that question. Her mom and her sister, Aunt Elaine, haven't seen eye to eye since—

ever! Melissa didn't know a single moment when the two exchanged cordial greetings, and she had no clue why.

"I know since Peter left that Christmas hasn't been easy for you," Betty, her mother, said sadly. "I just don't want you to be alone."

"Mom, I won't be alone," Melissa replied and wheeled the suitcases together to the door. She turned and looked back inside the house. "I have the kids," she said as she tried to skirt the issue.

"You know what I mean," her mother replied, and Melissa could almost see the frown marring her forehead, adding another line above her eyes.

"We won't be home anyway," Melissa said hesitantly.

"Where are you going?" Betty asked curiously.

Melissa sighed. "Yuletide Creek."

"Yuletide Creek?" Betty exclaimed, just as Gemma and Max started back down the stairs.

"Mom, can I bring my skateboard?" Max asked and dropped his suitcase at the bottom of the stairs.

"Yes," Melissa replied and squeezed her eyes shut as the noise echoed throughout the house. "What's with the noise?"

Gemma wheeled her carry-on to the door and opened it to go out. "Honey, take something else, will you?"

"I can't believe we're moving to hick village," Max complained. "I won't even have any friends there. What do kids do for fun over there?"

"Max, it's a normal town, with normal people and normal things to do," Melissa replied and slapped her hand to her forehead.

"Not like you have any friends here anyway." Gemma rolled her eyes and picked up a box off the floor.

"Look who's talking?" Max shouted back. "Who died

5

and made you prom queen?" he asked as his nose flared. "That's right! No one!"

"Kids! Can you just stop with the bickering already?" Melissa shouted to them.

"Why are you going to *her* house?" Betty asked her.

"Mom, she's my aunt. What's wrong with me going to her house? She's family." Melissa groaned as she felt the first pangs of a headache coming on.

"You know we've never gotten along," Betty complained.

"That's why *you're* not the one going. *I* am," Melissa told her. "Besides, it's not like we can come to you in Chiang Mai. The kids don't have passports, so we'll go where we can go. We all can't be expats and go where we want to, Mom. Besides, how is it over there?"

"I don't want to go either, Grandma," Max yelled when he realized who was on the phone.

Melissa's heart sank. It was as if she couldn't win. She failed at her marriage. She constantly felt like no matter how much she tried, she was failing as a mother. And then there were the fights with her mother.

"See?" Betty said in response to Max. "You and the kids should just stay home."

"We can't stay here," Melissa wailed. "I can't afford this place on my own. Plus, I think we could all do with a change, and Aunt Elaine has that big old house with just her. The children could use the space..."

"Space shmace," Betty mocked.

"Doesn't matter, Mom," Melissa replied in an infuriated voice. "We're going." And with that, the children's faces fell to the floor. "Now, get the other things into the car. We need to go."

"And you're going to live there?" Betty continued.

"Mom, what is it with you and Aunt Elaine, by the way?" Melissa asked for what felt like the millionth time since she'd known about their feuding.

"Why don't you ask her when you see her?" Betty huffed. "She's the one who wouldn't talk to me."

"But why?" Melissa asked and dragged the last suitcase to the door as Max picked up the single box on the floor.

"It's not important," Betty replied grumpily.

"Not important, yet you two haven't spoken in years?" Melissa asked and walked through the house again. She had the uncanny feeling she had forgotten something.

She didn't have much to go through. The house was primarily empty except for the old pianoforte she'd inherited when they'd moved in. There was also an additional bed frame that they didn't need, but other than that, the house was a ghost's haunt.

"Mom, I have to go now. I'll talk to you later," Melissa said as she pulled the door up after her and locked it.

Max was leaning against the car while Gemma sat in the front seat, staring at her phone. "Come on, let's go," she told them.

Max groaned and got in the back. "Can we stop for something to eat?"

"Seriously?" a flustered Melissa turned and asked. "We just walked out of the house."

"You packed up everything," he complained. "Nothing was there."

"You could have gotten something at the corner store down the street," she replied and glared at him through the rearview mirror. "I'm not going to stop yet."

"This is gonna be fun," Gemma replied sarcastically without looking up. "Six hours and nothing to do."

Melissa sighed and turned the key in the ignition. She was tired. She'd felt like that for the past five years— ever since Peter walked out. She was at her wit's end, trying to hold everything and everyone together. All she wanted was a break— a single moment in time when she wasn't worried about the children or stressed about her job.

She'd been a teacher for twenty years— worrying had been a part of her existence for as far back as she could remember. She could only hope that Yuletide Creek would cure some of that.

"Shoot!" Gemma cried and turned to her mother with a frightened look. "Mom, can we go back?"

"What? No! And I'd appreciate it if you two would just lay off it for once," she said as she gunned the car down the road. "I'm tired, and we're going, so knock it off!"

"I'm serious. Mom, I was charging the phone, and then I went downstairs and forgot about it. Can we go back?"

Melissa's face thinned to a slit as she tried to stifle the frustration. "Gemma, we're just going to have to get you a new charger."

"Mom, my battery's going to die!" Gemma wailed. "We'll be driving for six hours."

"You should have thought about that," Melissa told her and slid the car into the line of traffic heading for the interstate. "Too late now."

"Great," Gemma replied, and her head fell against the window with a bang. "This sucks!"

And all Melissa could think was, *you have no idea!*

Chapter Two

The last six hours dissolved like mist in the morning sun as soon as they crossed the sign that read *Welcome to Yuletide Creek.*

Max was snoozing in the back, and Gemma's head was resting against the window, her mouth half open.

"We're here, honey," Melissa said happily and glanced over at her.

She didn't move. "Hooray," she said less than enthusiastically and did a weak fist-pump.

Melissa smiled and ruffled her hair. "I promise it won't be as bad as you think. I know it's not a city, but you know, Yuletide Creek has its charms."

"Can't wait to see what that is," she moaned.

But as soon as the first lights appeared that signaled civilization, Melissa's heart warmed. "Look at that." She pointed and dipped her head to see better as the twinkling lights got brighter the closer they got.

Gemma's head slowly rose, and she looked at the glorious display of Christmastime in Yuletide Creek.

There were lights everywhere and in all sorts of

colors. They ran around the display cases in the shop windows, chasing each other like little red, green, and yellow horses in a miniature thoroughbred race.

Sal's Sip n' Dip had a giant Santa Claus outside that was rocking from side to side and ringing a bell. The store next to it had its competition in the form of a nutcracker guard pointing to the store, ushering everyone inside.

"Isn't that cute?" Melissa asked as she noticed the red-nosed Rudolph and friends inside the display case of the bakery.

"They sure know how to light up a town," Gemma commented, just as Max woke up.

"What's happening?" he asked and yawned.

"We're here," Melissa told him as she let the car glide into town at thirty miles an hour, just so she could take in the lights. "And it's awesome."

Her spirit was already lifted as she was surrounded by lights. Christmas was one of her favorite times of the year, and she felt like a child again. There wasn't a single store that didn't have some form of a tree, ornaments, bells, or dancing Santa Claus and prancing reindeer. Only the street was bare of Christmas lights and holiday cheer.

"That's a big tree for a small town," Gemma noted when they passed the town tree.

"It is," Melissa said.

The street she turned onto didn't let her down— it wasn't just Main Street that boasted the Christmas spirit. Every house had hanging lights dangling from the awnings or picket fences lined with a variety of lights. Some rooftops had sleighs with Santa Claus on them and lawns covered with candy canes, elves, and reindeer.

Nothing about Yuletide Creek seemed real— Melissa

felt as if she'd just walked onto the cover of a Hallmark card.

"This ought to be fun," Gemma said in her resident sarcastic voice. "Christmas without friends."

"Oh, come on. Don't tell me you don't feel even a little cheerful after seeing all of this," Melissa said as she slowed down and checked for the mailbox that would tell her which was Aunt Elaine's house. She remembered that the house was further back from the road and not like many of the others.

"Nope," Gemma answered.

Melissa ignored her and kept looking for the number. She was excited about what Aunt Elaine had done with the place and more so about the Christmas dinner, which she was already planning in her head. When the car rolled to a stop outside twenty-four, her mouth fell.

The fact that it was already dark made it glaringly obvious how much Aunt Elaine's house lacked the Christmas spirit. There wasn't a single light except for the pale glow of the stars above.

"Sheesh!" Melissa said as she turned the car onto the driveway. "What happened here?"

"So, in a lame town, we get the only house that's not decorated?" Max frowned and got out of the car. "I wish I could just leave."

Melissa clenched her jaw. "Do you have to be this insensitive all the time? Do either of you ever stop to ask me what I want or how I feel, huh? *This* is where we'll spend Christmas. Now, help me get the things out of the car, and I don't want either of you to go in there with all this attitude," Melissa warned. "We're going to enjoy the holidays. Is that too much to ask?"

They both sighed and proceeded to lift boxes out of

the car. "Can we just go inside? I'm tired," Gemma asked in a defeated tone.

"Go ahead," Melissa said as Aunt Elaine came onto the porch.

"Hello there!" she called to them and waved. "Need a hand?" she asked and tried to climb down the stone steps that led to the narrow walkway lined with smooth stones.

"No, we've got it," Melissa called to her.

"Are you sure?" she asked, stopping with one foot on the porch and the other on the first step.

"It's three of us. We'll manage," Melissa told her. But even as she said the words, she wasn't so sure. With all the bickering between Max and Gemma, and the constant questions and guilt trips set by her mother, Melissa was beginning to question if she'd ever had a happy anything at all. Not just Christmas.

She sighed and lugged the suitcase from the car, rolling it up the steps as she tried to avoid toppling it over the stones the wheels kept hitting.

Aunt Elaine hugged them all as soon as they met her on the porch. Even in the dark, her gray eyes twinkled, and her face lit up like it was its own Christmas tree. "I'm so happy to have all of you here," she said and squeezed Melissa especially tight. "Come in, come in," she said and beckoned them inside. Her dark coat rubbed against her calves as she led the way for Melissa and the two grumpy teenagers that followed.

But it wasn't just the outside of the house that had a gloomy look— the inside was just the same. It was as if Aunt Elaine had forgotten about Christmas. The house had a musty smell, and from what Melissa could tell, just from the mini-tour through the lower level of the house, Aunt Elaine only occupied one section of the house— a corner of the living room that housed a rocking chair and knitting apparatuses, and a small table with a tray. Melissa could tell she hardly ever moved from the spot.

"Now, you all go on up and get settled," the woman beamed, her gray hair under the silk scarf peeking out around her hairline. "And when you're done, I've got hot cocoa and cookies, and you can tell me all about the ride here." She didn't wait for an answer— she just hurried off to the kitchen.

"Okay, kids, come on," Melissa told the less than enthusiastic children. "Let's pick a room and unpack."

The upstairs bedrooms and layout were even worse than downstairs. The house was much too big for Aunt Elaine, and much of it had gone neglected. Their dreary looks were dampened even further when they saw the drab curtains and floral wallpaper adorning the rooms.

Luckily, they each had their own rooms, which made things a lot easier for Melissa. The house itself was beautiful, with ornate carvings over the fireplace and crystal chandeliers hanging over the dining table and the kitchen island. The wooden floor was in spectacular condition, and with some extra polish and some sprucing, the place would look brand new in no time.

Melissa didn't see the gloominess, and she wouldn't let anything dampen her spirits. She only saw the possibilities, and she'd make it a Christmas to remember.

With a new pep in her step, she washed up and made her way downstairs. It was a little after eight, so they still had some time before they needed to sleep.

"Good, you're all washed up and ready," Aunt Elaine said as she hurried to the kitchen. "Will the kids be down?"

"Who knows?" Melissa sighed and climbed onto the

barstool. "They've been giving me grief ever since they found out I was coming here."

Aunt Elaine laughed. "Just give them some time. They're only what, eighteen and fifteen?" she asked.

"Max is sixteen, actually," Melissa corrected her.

"Oh, wow. Time's going, isn't it?" she asked as she poured out two cups of cocoa for them. She picked up a tray of cookies wrapped in cling wrap and slid it over to Melissa. "Help yourself."

"Yeah, it is," Melissa replied and sipped from her cup. "Can't believe they're this old, and Gemma will be going to college soon. I'm going to be on my own in no time."

"Yes." Aunt Elaine sighed and stared off into space, her hands caressing the cup she probably was no longer feeling.

"It doesn't have to be that way for you, though," Melissa reminded her. "You have a sister. I don't. It was just me."

"I only have a sister by a technicality," she huffed and pulled her robe around her.

"But that's a choice. What could be so bad between you and Mom that you'd rather go through life without each other? I'd give anything for a sister."

"Be careful what you wish for," Aunt Elaine replied bitterly, and her lips twisted into a frown.

"What happened?" Melissa asked, even though she doubted she'd ever get an answer. She'd asked both her mother and aunt that question for years, and she was still clueless.

Aunt Elaine stared into her cup for a couple of minutes, and then she looked up, sporting a grin that illuminated her face. "I know the kids got off to a slow start, but they'll love it here."

Classic! That was what she always did— change the subject. "You and Mom are definitely sisters. And yeah, I hope they warm up. This gloomy attitude isn't going to cut it."

"There's tons for them to do at this time of year. There's the local skating rink, the movie theaters, and the shopping strip. Heck, they just need to meet other kids their age, and they'll be happy in no time. And there are tons of Christmas activities. We already had a few, but there's the tree gallery coming up. They'll love that."

"I hope so," Melissa replied.

"Hey, maybe they can help out at the local food bank," Aunt Elaine suggested.

Melissa raised her eyebrows. "My kids? At the food bank? Pretty sure they'd just scare off everyone else."

Aunt Elaine laughed. "You'd be surprised. It's Christmas, after all."

"Speaking of," Melissa interrupted her. "What happened here? Not even a bow?"

Aunt Elaine laughed again. "I'm an old woman with a bad back. Couldn't get up to that task."

"Guess it's my job now," Melissa grinned.

"Knock yourself out." She smiled. "I could use some extra Christmas cheer."

"Aunt Elaine, you said you had cookies, right?" Max asked as he suddenly appeared in the kitchen.

"Why, yes!" she replied excitedly. "Take as much as you want."

"Don't mind if I do," he said, leaning in to grab a handful.

"Save some for Gemma," Melissa said and slapped his hand away.

"She's watching her weight." He smirked and ran off again.

"And you said there was no hope," Aunt Elaine chuckled.

And Melissa's heart warmed. For the first time since she'd arrived, she felt as if life wasn't going to be so bad after all.

But she was afraid to think about how long that would last.

Chapter Three

Melissa's eyes opened, and instantly her heart quickened.

She remembered where she was and why she was there— a fresh start. Plus, it was almost Christmas, and she had a lot to do.

She got out of bed and ventured to the window. The property on which the house stood was vast. There were evergreen trees, pine trees, and an otherwise wooded wonderland of bare trees waiting for their spring leaves.

It resembled something from *Lord of the Rings,* and she smiled as she envisioned it being a bridge to a fairy world. She could feel the enthusiasm building in her, and she raced from her room to Gemma's as if she was the parent and Melissa was the child.

"Rise and shine!" Melissa said as she barged into the room.

"Mom," Gemma groaned and pulled the covers over her head. "Not now. I'm tired."

"Honey, it's morning, and we have a lot to do," Melissa said in an upbeat way.

"Like what? This isn't New York."

"So?" Melissa asked and tried to yank the covers back. "There are other things to do. It's almost Christmas. There's shopping, decorating the house, and going to Santa's village."

Gemma pulled the covers back and stared at her mother in disbelief. "Santa's village? Mom, I'm eighteen, not five. I don't believe in Santa Claus."

"When did you get so dull?" Melissa said as she got up. "Let's see what Max has to say."

"Good luck with that," she said and rolled her eyes as she pulled the covers over her.

Melissa hoped she'd have better luck with Max, but when she opened the room and saw him, already up, with his ear pods in and his eyes glued to his phone, she knew it was already a lost cause.

He glanced up and saw her standing by the door. "Hey, Mom."

"Max, how do you feel about going into town with me?" she asked.

"Huh?" he asked, even though he made no effort to remove his ear pods.

"Forget it." She waved and walked out of the room. She returned to her bedroom and changed into jeans and a sweatshirt. She pulled her hair to the back of her head in a ponytail before heading downstairs.

Aunt Elaine was already up and on the back porch, looking over her vast property. "I could get used to this," Melissa said as she joined her.

Aunt Elaine chuckled. "It's one of my favorite things to do."

"I bet it is," Melissa said as she got up and walked to

the front of the yard. "I haven't seen this house for so long." She walked around to the side of the house. It was painted in a soft yellow color, with white borders around the windows and doors. The large wraparound porch at the front could use a little paint, but it was still a handsome house.

Aunt Elaine had potted plants that hung from the edges of the porch which were now devoid of plants. The green expanse in the background gave the house a picturesque view, with the outline of the mountaintops dotting the canvas.

"All this house needs now is some holiday cheer," Melissa said and returned to the porch. But I'm going to need some help."

"Have at it," Aunt Elaine told her.

"First things first. We need a tree," she said excitedly. "Do you have decorations at all?"

"Not really. Just some old ornaments. You can make popcorn strings if you like. I believe I have popcorn."

Melissa groaned. "Ugh, Aunt Elaine, you're killing me."

The old woman chuckled. "What's an old woman to do?"

"Okay, fine. Tree. Ornaments. Done. Now to get these children up so they can come and pick out the tree. If they think they're going to sleep this Christmas away, they have another thing coming." And with fierce determination, she climbed up the stairs and pushed the doors in.

"Okay, everybody up!" she yelled. They started complaining, but Melissa simply pulled the covers off Gemma and took away Max's phone.

"Mom, come on," Max wailed. "I was in the middle of a game."

"And I just need some sleep." Gemma sighed as her hands fell to her sides.

"There's plenty of time to sleep later and to play video games. Right now, I'm going into town to pick out a tree and get some decorations. There's other stuff you kids can do when we get there, but we're getting out of the house today, so be ready in fifteen minutes."

"This isn't happening," Gemma replied in disbelief.

"It's something to do, isn't it?" Melissa turned and asked as they followed her like zombies. All that was left was for them to start foaming at the mouth.

"Going to pick out a Christmas tree," Gemma said and clumped down the stairs angrily. "Mom, we're not five anymore. We don't need a tree."

"Yeah," Max agreed.

Melissa looked at them both when she was at the bottom of the stairs. "Oh, so now you both want to agree on something?" She crossed her arms and glared at them.

"Yes!" they replied together and then looked across at each other and erupted into laughter.

"Nice to see you both coming around," Melissa said as she grabbed her purse. "Let's go. If we're lucky, we'll get a good tree."

"I still can't believe we're doing this," Max groaned when they walked to the car.

The day was warm, despite the frost that had settled overnight. A cool breeze gently tossed Gemma's hair as it swished against her shoulders.

"This is a nice house," Melissa said as she sat in the car and looked at the faded-yellow exterior of Aunt Elaine's home.

"Yeah," Max grunted. "If you want to go to *Terabithia.*"

Gemma chuckled. "You're not wrong."

"What's he talking about?" Melissa asked and backed the car out of the driveway.

"Goblins and fairies." Gemma giggled. "The house does look enchanted. I think a Christmas tree and decorations are going to ruin the natural appeal."

Melissa laughed. "Very funny," she said. "Not gonna work."

But they were sort of right. As the house grew smaller, it reminded her of those mansions hidden behind giant walls with creeping vines— like something from King Arthur's realm.

"We're going to have so much fun," Melissa said as the car rolled down Main Street. But even as she was saying it, she struggled to believe it. They had no friends, and for children of the same parents, Gemma and Max couldn't be more different.

The car was deadly silent as Melissa tried desperately to follow the GPS to the local tree lot. It was the only one in town, but how many tree lots did one town need for a season? She was trying to cheer up and pull her children in.

"Who wants to listen to music?" she asked as she touched the dial.

"Nope!" Gemma said and instantly turned it off again.

"Why not?" Melissa turned to her and asked with a look of dismay plastered on her face.

"I'm not in the mood to listen to *Jingle Bells* or *Chestnuts Roasting on an Open Fire.*"

Max chuckled. "Got that right."

"Oh, come on," Melissa groaned. "Are you two my children? Can we just have a nice day today like normal people and do the things normal people do at Christmastime?"

She sighed as disappointment began to take root in her. It seemed as if she, of all the people at Aunt Elaine's house, was the only one who cared about Christmas. It was up to her to inject the Christmas spirit into her entire family, and it seemed more and more to be a gargantuan task.

She raked her hand through her hair and gripped the wheel with the other. She barely saw the road— she felt like an automaton.

Then, she heard a loud hissing sound as the car swung from one side of the lane to the other. She felt as if she was driving on loose stones, and then she realized what was wrong.

"Are you kidding me?" she cried out loud as she pulled the car over to the side of the road.

"What's wrong?" Max scooted forward and asked.

"We have a flat," Melissa said and got out of the car. Sure enough, the right passenger tire was busted.

"Great!" Gemma groaned. "As if this day couldn't get any worse.

"It's okay," Melissa said and tried to be as optimistic as she could. "I can do this."

"Do what?" Gemma asked and stared at her as if she had horns in her head.

"Change the flat," she said less than confidently as she knelt beside the tire and surveyed it. "Dad taught me a long time ago, but it's like riding a bicycle."

Gemma gave her a blank stare. "Yeah. Right. You change a tire."

"I can," she said and walked around to the trunk. She popped it open and lifted out the spare. "Easy peasy."

Gemma rolled her eyes and walked to the other side of the car. She leaned against it and fished out her phone.

Max walked over to the side of the road, pulled his hood over his head, and kicked at the turf. He looked like a bored child on a playground.

When Melissa knelt on the cold asphalt with the spare donut under one arm and stared at the jack, doubt overwhelmed her. Her dad had taught her a long time, but for even more years, twenty, she'd had a husband for that sort of thing. But she was determined to get it done. She didn't need a man.

But whatever she'd learned, she'd completely forgotten. She placed the jack under the car, sliding it from the front to the back of the tire, not quite sure where exactly to place it. She sort of remembered it should be at the back, so she positioned it and started pumping on the lever. When the car was lifted, she turned to Gemma and grinned.

"See? Step one, done!"

Gemma rolled her eyes, but Melissa was proud of her small accomplishment. The next step wasn't as encouraging. She hit her hand on the ground a couple of times when she tried to get the lug nuts off the wheel.

She was getting frustrated, and so were the children, when a red Ford pickup drove down the street and stopped in front of her car. She noticed the scruffy, bearded man that stepped out and walked over to her.

He was wearing a long-sleeved denim shirt with matching pants and work boots. He was handsome, in a rugged sort of way, but Melissa tried not to focus on that.

"I'm fine, thanks," she told him before he even offered his hand.

"Is that so? When I see a lady out here changing a tire, I'm not just going to keep driving, ma'am," he said in a kind voice.

"I appreciate it, but I can do it," she retorted, desperate to prove she could handle it.

"Ma'am, are you sure?" he asked and raised his brows. "I think you're turning that the wrong way."

"I can do it!" Melissa said. "I don't need a man."

"Okay!" he said and held his hands up in defeat as he backed away.

Melissa huffed and started turning the bar in the opposite direction, but even as she did, the iron hopped off the nut, hit the pavement, and cracked. It was rusting, and she hadn't paid much attention to that.

She clenched her jaw just as the stranger chuckled. "Seems you need help after all."

"It's fine, mister," Gemma walked over and told him. "I called roadside assistance."

Melissa wasn't sure if Gemma was lying, and for a second, she thought about taking his offer of help since she no longer had the jack. But only for a second. She couldn't take it— not after the way she'd rejected him.

"Okay," he said and walked away. "My sandwich is getting cold anyway."

Melissa watched his lean stagger to the truck before she got up and turned to Gemma. "Thanks for stepping in. I thought he'd never go away. That was a pretty neat con."

"Oh, it wasn't a con," Gemma told her. "I called road-side assistance."

"You what?" Melissa asked in disbelief.

"Good thing I did too," Gemma said and pointed at the broken jack still on the road.

Melissa wasn't sure if she should be grateful that she had or disappointed at her lack of faith in her. But at that point, it didn't even matter anymore.

Chapter Four

I t wasn't until an hour later, after navigating between Gemma's and Max's attitudes, that the roadside assistance team finally showed up. Melissa was a second away from tearing out her hair.

"Finally!" Gemma groaned when the truck pulled up to them.

It didn't take very long for them to be on their way, and more than anything else, the children wanted to return home. Melissa ignored them as she watched the GPS to the tree lot.

"Not much of a day if we just get a flat and go back home, would it?" she asked and slammed her door shut. "Now, I've had it with the attitude. Let's just do this."

"Fine," Gemma replied and hopped out of the car. "First tree we see, and that's it."

Melissa rolled her eyes and walked off with the two moping behind her. She'd pretty much given up on them — there was no getting the Christmas spirit into them, and it was slowly sapping it from her.

They walked onto the lot where several pine trees of

varying sizes were spread out in front of them. The lot had faux snow bedding, giving the place a woodsy vibe. The rich scent of pine permeated Melissa's senses, and just like that, she was back in Santa Claus mode.

"How about this one?" Gemma asked and showed her a ten-foot tree. "Looks about right."

"Not bad." Melissa nodded. "But we just got here. Let's see the rest of the place first."

"Mom, I don't think we *all* had to come for this," Max groaned. "Can I go wait in the car?"

"No!" Melissa told him. "We're doing this together. As a family."

Max shoved his hands deep into his pockets and sulked. "This sucks!" he grumbled under his breath.

"Tell me about it," Gemma agreed. "I don't see what the big deal is. We hardly do anything together anyway."

Melissa was feeling more defeated by the minute. It seemed as if the universe was against her. Her children had been giving her attitude all morning. She had a flat on the way to getting a Christmas tree. All she wanted was for them to be happy. Ever since their father walked out, everything had been different. She'd worked harder than ever before to keep the family together, even when she was falling apart.

Gemma would be in college soon, which meant, in a way, she was going to lose her too. And Max wasn't that far behind. She just wanted one thing to go right even if it was just picking out a darn Christmas tree.

She walked off, leaving them standing by the ten-foot tree. There were many different colored trees and some faux-white ones in the center. She imagined how the lot would look from an aerial view, and she smiled, completely ignoring the children.

She walked around the outer edges of the pine wall and turned to the edge toward the center when she looked to her right, and the smile instantly disappeared from her face. She spotted the stranger in his denim suit, wearing a bright grin as he conversed with a middle-aged woman in a black coat.

"Okay," Melissa said to herself and veered to the left. She didn't want to run into him. Her earlier embarrassment was enough. She'd been rude, and she knew it, but she hadn't thought about the fact that she'd ever run into him again.

"Mom, what are you doing?" Gemma asked.

She jumped and turned. "Nothing," she replied. She'd been trying to keep an eye on the gentleman, just to make sure she didn't meet him. "Just looking at the trees."

"Can we just go get an attendant or something? I want to go. There's nothing here to do," Max whined.

"Fine," Melissa snarled. She was just about ready to leave too. It didn't seem as if the stranger was going to leave any time soon.

She turned to walk away and walked right into him as he suddenly appeared from behind a tree. "Oh." He smiled when he saw her. "Can I help you?"

Melissa glowered at him. He had the nerve. "Mister, I'm not sure what kind of vibe you're getting from me, but I'm not into your little game. I didn't need your help on the street, and I don't need it now. I can certainly pick out a tree by myself."

"Uh but have you?" he asked and knitted his brow.

She crossed her arms. "What does it matter to you? Do you go around town asking everyone if they need help? I saw you earlier with that other woman. Did you help her?"

"I did," he said with pride and rubbed his hands together as he rocked back on his heels. "And I'm pretty sure I can help you too."

"I doubt it," she said and turned to the children. "Let's go."

She brushed past him, intent on wrapping up her deal with the tree and leaving. She'd had enough for one day. She noticed a woman as she was walking away and stopped her.

"Hey, do you know who's in charge? I'm new in town and don't know anyone, and I don't think I see an attendant," she said as she glanced around.

"Oh, sure," the woman said and turned. She clutched the purse under her arm, her silver hair showing around the edges of her woolen hat. "He was just right over there," she said.

Melissa looked in the direction the woman was looking, hoping to spot someone wearing a store bib or something resembling a uniform. She came up empty.

"There he is," she said gaily and pointed.

Melissa turned, and her breath caught in her throat when she saw that the woman was pointing at the stranger in the denim outfit, who was staring right at them with a smirk.

Oh, you've got to be kidding me!

"Thank you," she said to the woman, even as Gemma and Max started snickering.

"This ought to be awkward." Gemma laughed.

"Ugh!" Melissa groaned and walked away. "I'm not going back over there."

"Why not?" Gemma asked and pulled on her arm. "Mom, you got us to come out here to get a tree, and now that we're here, you just want to leave?"

"Fine by me," Max said and walked off.

"No!" Gemma exclaimed. "We're getting that tree."

Melissa tightened her lips and spoke through clenched teeth. "I'm not going over there to ask him for help."

"It's not asking for help, Mom. It's buying a tree. There's a difference."

"Not really. Can you imagine how much he'd gloat if I had to walk up to him and ask him to help me with buying a tree? Didn't you notice the conversations before?"

"Yes, but I don't know why you're so sensitive all of a sudden," Gemma whined as she followed her mother, who was heading for the door.

"I'm not being sensitive!" Melissa replied harshly.

"Then go and just get the tree, so we don't have to come back," Gemma coaxed her. "I know you, and if we go back home without the tree, then you're going to want to come back."

"There must be another place where we can get a tree," Melissa insisted. "I'll look."

"But Mom, we're already here!" Gemma cried and pointed at the store. "You just wasted our morning."

"I'm not going back in there," she told them, "and that's it! Now let's go."

"Hey!" someone called to her from the door.

She turned and saw the same stranger flagging her down and jogging over to her. "What?"

"I thought you wanted the tree," he said with concern in his eyes.

"I'm good, thanks," she said and turned to open her car.

"What's the problem?" he probed.

"Look!" she snapped. "I'm just trying to have a nice Christmas with my children. Do you mind?" She wasn't even sure why she was giving him attitude. Maybe she was already chock-full of all the disappointment and annoyance she could take for a day. "I don't need help from *you!*"

He crossed his arms. "You know, I've come across a lot of rude people in my day, but you have nothing over them. All I was doing, twice now," he said and held up his index and middle fingers, "was trying to help. Are you allergic to it?"

He had a scorned look that made Melissa's chest tighten. "If I don't need your help, all you have to do is find someone else. Why do you keep following me around? I already said no!"

"Oh, god," Gemma said and covered her face. "Please just take me now."

Melissa heard her whisper and glanced back at her and Max, who was standing around, staring at the sky and likely pretending he wasn't there.

"I get it," the man said and tipped his hat as he retreated. "That's what you get for being nice. Have a great Christmas!"

He turned and walked away, and Melissa was left feeling less than the ground she was standing on. It didn't help when she saw the disappointed looks on her children's faces.

"Mom, you didn't have to be mean," Gemma said as she got into the car.

"I wasn't trying to be mean, but it was getting creepy how he kept showing up," she argued.

"Yeah, but it wasn't like he was following us or

anything. He was driving past on the street, and this is *his* store," Gemma pointed out.

"Let's just go," Melissa said and started the car.

She couldn't deny how lousy she felt. They'd wasted the entire morning driving to the store for nothing. And she was ashamed of her behavior. Her pride had let her leave the store without a tree. But somehow, she knew it was more than that.

For two decades, she'd let a man rule over her, telling her what to do and not do. She'd given up all her independence from the day she was married, and for what? He'd taken everything she had to offer and then walked out on her.

She wasn't going to give another man that chance. She would prove to the world that she was capable of doing anything on her own. She could change her tire. She could pick out a tree. She could fly a shuttle to the moon.

She stared at the long stretch of road in front of her that led back to the gravelly path that would take them back to Aunt Elaine's. The entire ride back to the house, neither Max nor Gemma said a word. They didn't complain or bicker, and Melissa knew she had herself to thank for that.

She also knew that she wouldn't get them to go with her to get another tree. One way or another, she was on her own, and she sighed as the car turned off the main road. She couldn't see it being a merry Christmas after all.

Chapter Five

Melissa wanted to get a tree, but she knew she'd lost her helpers when, as soon as she pulled into the driveway, they both leaped out of the car as if it was on fire.

She sat in the driver's seat still, thinking about her next move. She stared at the only house in a three-mile radius that didn't have a string of lights wrapping around the house. Or a Santa Claus on the porch and reindeer on the lawn. What kind of Christmas could they hope to have without a single bell or ribbon?

Melissa took out her phone and started searching for local tree lots. She must have missed one. They were trees, for crying out loud. Someone else must be selling them. Or maybe there were some faux pine ones in a department store.

She didn't see any obvious stores like Ian's tree lot, which meant she was left with finding another solution. She backed out of the driveway and drove toward Main Street. The first department store she spotted was filled with all the Christmas goodies she could imagine. Faux elves skipped in the display cases, Santa Claus swayed by the door, nutcracker guards lined inside the doors, and the walls were covered with streamers and lights. Bows, ribbons, and bells adorned the countertops, and garlands made serpentine loops around the wooden frames.

It was like standing inside Christmas heaven.

"Merry Christmas," a rose-faced woman said as she approached Melissa. She was wearing a red bib that matched her lipstick.

"Oh, hi. Merry Christmas," Melissa replied. "Please tell me you have a Christmas tree left in store," Melissa groaned.

"Sorry," the woman replied. "We didn't get any this year. Did you check over at Ian's? He should have some."

"Thank you," Melissa said and turned around. Her smile instantly disappeared when she pushed the door to exit. She couldn't tell the attendant she'd already been to Ian's.

She drove to three other stores, but no one had even a five-foot faux pine tree. And she got the same direction from all of them. She was ashamed of her earlier interactions with who she then knew to be Ian. She wasn't sure she wanted to show her face there again. But getting everyone in the spirit of Christmas was already hard at the house. Without a Christmas tree, it would be next to impossible.

"I thought you'd gone back for the tree," Aunt Elaine greeted her when she opened the door.

"Couldn't find one," Melissa said grumpily and sat on the barstool. She slipped her hat off and started unbuttoning.

Aunt Elaine cocked her head to the side. "You couldn't find any, or you got into a little trouble?"

Melissa blushed and turned her head away. "I guess. But I'm not going back there. It's too embarrassing."

"How? Ian's a pretty decent guy. I doubt he'd be offended by whatever," Aunt Elaine defended.

Melissa narrowed her eyes. "What did Gemma tell you?"

She chuckled and waved off Melissa. "Nothing. Just that he tried to help, and you were being weird."

"I don't know what happened, Auntie," she said to the woman. "It's like I was a whole other person. I had a flat, and he offered to help, and I wouldn't let him. I don't even know why. Maybe pride. I just wanted to prove I could do it."

"But you didn't," Aunt Elaine pointed out as she slid a plate over to Melissa. It had a slice of apple pie that smelled like the best thing she'd ever smelled, and instantly she began to salivate. She'd forgotten she hadn't eaten all morning.

"Nope," Melissa replied. "And now, I can't just waltz in there grinning as if nothing happened," Melissa said and cut a piece of the pie. Her eyes closed as feelings of euphoria swept over her, and she moaned. "You have got to teach me how to make this," she said with a full mouth.

"In time," Aunt Elaine said and patted her hand.

The fork clattered to the plate when Melissa was done eating, and she sighed. "What am I going to do? We need a tree, and to get some decorations up. I was so out of it I went to the department stores searching for a tree and forgot to pick up the other ornaments and stuff I needed."

"Well," Aunt Elaine said and padded over to her. Her hair was out and showed signs of gray, but not as much as Melissa would have thought. They looked more like highlights than actual signs of aging. Her eyes were filled with crow's feet— also signs of a happy life, and she wondered if she'd have that happy face when she turned sixty.

"Yeah?" Melissa asked when she didn't say anything else.

"I mean, I'm not sure if it's any good, but there was a fake tree under the crawl space. It might still be there if you want to check," she said and shrugged.

She looked pessimistic about the prospects of the tree being in good condition, but the possibility that it could be was enough for Melissa. "Where?" she asked with wide eyes and instantly slid off the stool.

"Let me show you," Aunt Elaine offered and shuffled to the back door, her thick house dress rubbing against her ankles.

She pointed to a small, mesh wooden barrier that Melissa could lift to gain access. "In there. But I can't promise it'll be what you imagine."

"Let me be the judge of that," Melissa replied excitedly as she hurried over to the door. She lifted it and climbed down the two steps that led to the space. It was dry and musty, and an overwhelming smell overpowered her and elicited a throat-ripping sneeze.

"You alright down there?" Aunt Elaine asked from the porch.

"Just great," Melissa replied and looked around. She kept her hand under her nose to limit the dust particles she'd inhaled and blinked hard as her eyes adjusted to the limited lighting. She looked around, but she didn't immediately notice the tree. Boxes were lying around, a few pieces of broken furniture, and some broken sheets of plywood.

She was beginning to lose heart when she noticed the

extensive coverage in the corner on the ground. A dusty, white sheet was draped over something, and her heartbeat quickened when she pulled back the sheet and saw the prickly, pine thistles.

"Yes!" she hissed and pulled the sheet aggressively off the tree. Her heart soared as she reached down to pull it. She grabbed the base just as a rat scurried over her hand. Melissa screamed and fell backward hard onto her bottom as the animal dashed under the tree. That wasn't all. Before she could move, fluttering wings headed right for her, and she shielded her face as a bat brushed against her arm.

"No!" she screamed and dashed to the door. She didn't care if the tree could work. There was no way she was bringing that into the house. She'd rather burn it first.

"Is everything alright?" Aunt Elaine asked from just outside the trap door. "I heard a scream."

"Darn rat. And a bat!" Melissa hissed as she climbed out of the opening. "Ugh!" she said as she shivered and hugged herself.

"I guess that means you won't use that tree then." Aunt Elaine chuckled as she walked behind her.

"Not funny," Melissa groaned and pulled the screen door open. "We still don't have a tree."

"You could if you wanted to," she said and looked at Melissa as if she was looking over the rim of glasses.

"Auntie, I can't go back there," Melissa moaned. "It's too embarrassing."

"Well," she said, "there are ways to get to a man."

Melissa cocked her head in wonderment. "Please tell."

"I happen to know for a fact that Ian has a sweet

tooth. Maybe you could butter him up a little so you don't look as bad?"

Melissa laughed. "Are you saying I should bribe the man?"

"Not bribe. Just extend an olive branch in the form of treats. Play nice."

Melissa sighed. But what other option did she have? It was either that or forfeit Christmas. "Okay, fine. But this had better work. I don't want to look like the bad guy three times."

Aunt Elaine snickered. "Here, let me make you a nice basket. It's the least I can do since I can't help with the decorating or anything."

Aunt Elaine wrapped some muffins, apple pie, and mince pie, along with a bottle of hot apple cider, and handed it to Melissa. "This ought to work."

Melissa was less than optimistic when she left the house. It didn't matter that she was bringing treats— she still had to face the man. Her heart pounded as she pulled into the parking lot. She didn't know the first thing to say, and she didn't want to walk up and just hand him the basket. It was all touch and go still.

But she had to do it for the sake of Christmas.

She sucked in a deep breath and, with the basket draped over her arm, she went in search of Ian. She spotted him before he saw her, with a woman and her teenage son. He was pointing at a tree and saying something she couldn't hear.

Watching him only increased her anxiety, but her fascination for him started to take root. He was a handsome man— that much she already knew. But she liked the way his face lit up when he laughed and how kind his voice was. She hung back until he was through with three different sets of customers, and she observed that he was much more pleasant than she'd given him credit for. She was the one who'd been acting like an idiot.

But she couldn't delay her shame any longer. With no one else distracting him, she knew she had to go to him. She started walking toward him when he turned and saw her. Instantly he held up his hands. "Okay, I surrender!"

Melissa smiled weakly. "I guess I deserve that," she said as she watched his eyes dip to the basket on her arm.

"Is that...?"

"Oh, yes," she said, almost forgetting her bribe. "This is for you."

He narrowed his eyes at her. "You're a strange woman."

"I know," she said and blushed. "I was a little overwhelmed earlier, and my kids were being bratty. I wanted to give them a nice Christmas, but they didn't appreciate it, and they were bickering the whole time, so when you stopped to ask me if I wanted help, I snapped, but it wasn't about you. I was on my own for the first time in a long time, and I just didn't know how to accept help from anyone and..."

"Whoa!" Ian stopped her and chuckled. "I get it. You don't need to overshare right now."

Melissa blushed. "Oh, sorry. I got carried away. But in any case, this is for you. A peace offering." She handed the basket to him.

"Hmm, it smells delicious," he said and took it. "Tell you what?" he said and made a sweeping gesture of the store. "How about I help you to pick out that tree."

"I would love that," she said and locked her fingers in front of her like a lovestruck teenager., swaying as she did. The only thing left for her to do was bat her eyes at him.

He laughed. "Let me go and set this down somewhere safe, and then we'll get you that tree. Free of charge."

"Oh no, you don't have to do that," Melissa said hastily.

"I insist," he told her and winked. "I'll call it starting over with a clean slate. Let bygones be bygones."

"Okay. Thank you," Melissa said. Relief washed over her as she watched Ian walk away. Their exchange hadn't been as bad as she thought it would have been. He was much nicer, as Aunt Elaine had said. And not so bad to look at.

But that wasn't a thought she was willing to entertain. For the moment, a Christmas tree would do. She wasn't sure she'd ever be ready for anything else from anyone.

But the warm feeling in her belly when she saw him returning was enough to give her second thoughts.

Chapter Six

"Do you need help bringing the tree home?" Ian asked her when she'd picked out the ten-footer she'd fallen in love with.

"That would be great. I doubt I'll be able to lug this into the house on my own."

"Okay, give me a couple of minutes, and I'll be right with you," he said and hurried off.

Melissa returned to the parking lot to wait on Ian, but her heart kept racing. She got more anxious, and her eyes darted all over the yard in search of him. When his truck pulled around the side of the building, a lump instantly formed in her throat.

What's wrong with me?

"Ready?" he asked.

He'd already loaded the tree into his pickup. "Yeah, follow me," she told him and hopped into her car.

She was over the moon because she'd finally gotten a tree. It would cost her a couple of hundred dollars, but she needed every piece of ornament to adorn the house and yard. And she wasn't going to do it alone. She'd find something even Aunt Elaine could do.

"You're kidding," Ian said when he bounded out of the truck at the yard. "You live here?"

"Only just recently moved into town," Melissa told him.

"Hello, Ian." Aunt Elaine waved as she came onto the porch.

He placed his hands on his hips and started laughing. "Well, if it ain't a small world. Hi, Elaine."

"I see you got my niece that tree," she beamed. "Here, bring it in."

"Way ahead of you," he said and smiled at Melissa. "Related to Elaine. I knew that apple pie tasted familiar. She's been bribing me with that thing for years."

Melissa laughed. "I bet she has. I'm sure it works every time."

"Like a charm," Ian said as he started hauling the tree from the back of his truck. "Seems she taught you the family way."

Melissa giggled and blushed. "I didn't know."

"I don't mind." He winked. "Can you get the other end there?" he asked and pointed to the tip of the tree. "I don't want it scratching the floor."

"Oh, sure," Melissa said and hurried to the other end.

They got the tree inside and positioned it by the fireplace. Melissa was excited as she imagined how it would look laden with ornaments and popcorn strings, ribbons, bows, and bells.

"Okay, if there's nothing else, I best be going," Ian said and walked back to the door.

Melissa followed him. "Thanks again, Ian. This was

really nice of you, especially after how awful I was to you."

He waved her off. "Don't mention it. Have a happy holiday."

"Thanks. You too," she said as she stood by the door, watching him leave.

"I think he has the hots for you," Aunt Elaine whispered in her ear.

"Oh, gross, Auntie." Melissa laughed. "You and I are not talking men."

Aunt Elaine shuffled back into the house. "Why not? We always have."

"Yeah, but not when it's you trying to play cupid with me," Melissa told her.

"You had a lousy husband. Nothing's wrong with hooking you up with someone nicer," Aunt Elaine insisted.

"Maybe, but I'm not ready for any of that yet. What I do want to do is get this tree set up. Christmas is in two weeks, and this house looks like it's getting ready to be sold."

Aunt Elaine chuckled. "Fine. I'll get out of your way. I have a few decorations in the coat closet by the back door."

"Great!" Melissa said and hurried off. At least something was coming up awesome. The day wasn't totally wasted after all.

She found the single box Aunt Elaine mentioned, which meant she still needed to get way more items. Ian had been nice enough to trim the tree, so that was one less thing to do. She returned to the heavily decorated department store and found a carload of items. When she returned, it was early evening, but she wanted to get as much done as she could.

Which meant she'd need help.

Aunt Elaine was sitting by the fireplace knitting when Melissa walked back inside. She could still feel the rush of adrenaline as she walked up the stairs. She could also feel her achy muscles dying for a chance to rest. She'd been very active all day, more than she'd been in a while.

She hoped Gemma wouldn't give her attitude and that, for once, something with her would be easy. She neared Gemma's door when she noticed it was slightly ajar. She was about to knock when Gemma spoke.

"I don't know how to tell her that," she said.

Melissa froze. Her hand slowly moved to her side, but something forced her to stay outside the door. She realized Gemma was on the phone. It wasn't a habit of hers to eavesdrop, which was even weirder for her.

"I know," Gemma said as her voice dipped lower. "She's probably going to kill me when she finds out."

Melissa clamped her hand to her chest. She wasn't sure why she should be worried. She didn't even know what Gemma was talking about or about whom.

"I know, I'll have to tell her, but you know, Mom. She's going to flip."

So, she is talking about me.

Melissa's heart started to race, but she didn't want to assume the worst. She wasn't even sure what the worst would be anyway. Though they acted spoiled on occasion, they were largely good kids. Whatever it was she was struggling with, she'd tell her sooner or later. At that moment, she had only one concern, and that was getting ready for Christmas.

She sucked in a deep breath and knocked on the door.

"Gotta go," Gemma told her caller. "Mom?"

Melissa poked her head through the door. "How'd you know it was me?"

"You knock the same way," Gemma replied as if that was a known, universal fact. "What's up? And no, I'm not going back with you to get the tree. You already messed that up."

"That's fine. I already went back on my own and got one. *And* decorations. Now I need help setting things up," Melissa said and edged closer to Gemma. "So, how about it?"

Gemma fell back on the bed. "Can I skip that?"

"Come on," Melissa begged. "I can't do it alone. It's just a couple of lights, and if we do this today, then we won't have to worry about it ever again."

"Until next Christmas," Gemma groaned.

"That's a year away. I don't ask you for anything, Gemma," Melissa said as frustration set in. "Just this one thing, and only because I can't do it by myself."

"But Mom, you *don't* have to do that," Gemma rose onto her elbow and whined. "I think this is silly and unnecessary. There's no kid in the house."

"I want to do it," Melissa said and tapped her chest. "It's important to me."

Gemma sighed loudly. "Fine."

"Thank you," Melissa replied and got up. "Now let's see about Max."

Max was sitting on the bed, his back against the wall and his phone in his hand. He was wearing his ear pods, and his eyes didn't shift from the phone when Melissa walked in.

"Max?" Nothing. "Max!" she said louder.

He glanced up and then tapped the screen. "Mom?"

"Can I get some help downstairs, please?"

He stared at her for a couple of seconds. "Now?"

"Yes. Now," Melissa replied. "Time's wasting, and I just want to get this done as soon as possible.

Max looked over her shoulder at Gemma, who shrugged at him. "Okay," he said and rolled his eyes.

"Good," Melissa said and walked back out. She only planned on decorating the living area, stringing lights on the porch and setting some elves on the walkway. She'd also ordered a Santa Claus that she'd place by the door. It wouldn't be the best house on the block, but it'd look a whole lot better than the nothing it was currently sporting.

"Okay, help me get some things out of the car," she said when they hit the landing.

Their shoulders sagged all the way to the car and back, and several times they returned with solo items, making more trips than they needed to. Melissa tried to ignore them.

"Alright, who wants to string the popcorn?" she asked in the deafening silence. "Fine. I will. But Max, you can get the lights. Gemma, you can start hanging the ornaments."

Melissa thought that task would have been easy enough until she saw the cluster of ornaments in the front and hardly anything in the back.

"Gemma, no," she said and walked over. "Spread them out. We have bells and ribbons to hang as well."

"Ugh!" Gemma groaned and started pulling ornaments down.

Melissa returned to her task of wrapping the banister with garland. When she was done, she pulled the stepladder to the wall at the front of the house, behind the door. Her plan was to make a garland and ribbon border, to which she'd add lights afterward. She was going up the ladder when she noticed Max getting tangled up in the lights.

"Max!" she said and walked over to him. "It's not that complicated."

He lifted some over his head and walked out of the entangled mess. "I thought they'd come out of the boxes better than that."

Melissa sighed. She took out the colored lights and placed them by the tree. "Okay, use the white ones to wrap around the banister. We'll use the colored ones on the tree."

She returned to her task, but several times she had to stop to correct Gemma or to fix the lights Max had strung. It wasn't hard to tell they were robotically going about the Christmas decorations. Their hearts weren't in it. Melissa had hoped that by being around all the candy canes, lights, and whistles, they'd at least have gotten a spark.

But after an hour of constantly fixing what they were doing, she gave up. "You know what?" she asked and took the box of bows from Gemma. "I'll just do the rest by myself."

Gemma looked hurt. "Are you sure?"

"I'm taking more time correcting your mistakes than I'd take if I were doing this myself. So, if you want to go do something else, be my guest."

Max was already halfway up the stairs by the time she was done talking. Aunt Elaine walked out of the kitchen and joined her in the living room. "I see you're coming along."

"Not as much as I'd have liked," Melissa said and

sighed. "The tree still needs to get done, and then there's all of this."

"It doesn't have to be a one-day task, you know," Aunt Elaine said. "Here, let me string the popcorn for you."

"Thanks." Melissa smiled, grateful for any help she could get. Then she plopped down on the sofa. "Does any of this make sense?" she asked and gestured to the tree. "I mean, I'm doing this for them and us, so we can have a nice Christmas, like a real family. Is that so hard?"

"Nothing's wrong with that, honey," Aunt Elaine told her and rubbed her shoulder. "But they're not little kids anymore. Maybe you should find out from them what they'd like to do and stop frustrating yourself by trying to make them like things they don't."

"I guess you're right," Melissa agreed. "But it's too late. I already have this tree. And Christmas would just feel weird without it."

"The tree is nice, but I'm just glad you're here with me." Aunt Elaine smiled.

"Me too," Melissa replied. "Now, if we could get my kids on the same page."

Aunt Elaine chuckled. "One miracle at a time."

Chapter Seven

Melissa's joints ached when she woke up the following morning. She'd gotten most of the Christmas decorations up. All that was left were a few items to add to the front porch. She was contemplating getting some tokens for the yard or maybe some lights for the picket fence, but she'd think about it later.

The sun was barely peeking over the horizon, warming the land. She watched the rays quickly spreading over the bare treetops from the window. She had enough time to go for her morning run. She didn't have a route yet, so she figured she'd head into town. It should be empty since none of the shops were open.

She zippered her jacket and headed downstairs. The house was quiet, and she smiled as she surveyed her handiwork— the house was coming along nicely. In a week, they wouldn't know what hit them.

She stepped outside into the frosty morning chill. It was colder than she imagined it would be, and she shivered and contemplated going back inside. But to do what?

"Fine," she mumbled. "Do your worst."

And she started down the street. It was one of her favorite things to do. Running calmed her and allowed her to think. Or get things off her chest. It was relaxing and soothing, and it seemed all her troubles melted away with each step. She was a lover of nature, and she got to see nature at its best when the rest of the world was still and there was nothing but peaceful bliss.

She tapped the play button on her phone, and her favorite station started playing indie pop. She loved the up-tempo beat when she was running, and it tended to carry her further than she planned.

Before she knew it, she was on Main Street, and she was barely breaking a sweat. She stopped outside a store to check the time. She'd been running for half an hour, and her throat was beginning to burn. She walked around, shaking her legs to keep them from tightening up on her before she started running again.

She didn't notice the store she was standing outside of until she turned back around. It was an old antique shop with the most beautiful display of dancing elves and prancing reindeer.

"Oh, nice," she said as she looked over the various Christmas images— the Santa Claus with the bell, the nutcracker, paraphernalia of jewelry boxes, trinkets, snow globes, and vials that added to the strange yet pleasant viewing.

It was then she started to pay closer attention to the other items on display in the other stores. It was like walking through a Santa village. She'd seen the displays in passing but just walking by, listening to the bells, touching the pine cones hanging from the awnings and on the Christmas trees outside.

And then there was the giant tree in the center of town, laden with multicolored ornaments, ribbons, and lights. She was fully imbibed with the Christmas spirit. She only wished her children had the same experience.

Her legs were getting lazy, so Melissa decided it was time to run the distance back. It took her less than thirty minutes to do so, and she was breathless, sweaty, and thirsty by the time she burst through the door.

"Oh, where did you go?" Aunt Elaine asked when she spotted her.

Melissa held up a finger and headed for the case of water in the pantry. She guzzled down a couple of ounces before she was able to talk. "Running."

"I reckoned," Aunt Elaine said and motioned to her outfit. "I used to do that when I was younger. Wish I could, but these old bones…"

Melissa laughed. "I know what you mean. I might have to give it up in a couple of years."

"Seems you have a lot more in you," Aunt Elaine said. "I'm about to make breakfast," she said and opened the cupboard door. Her hair was uncovered, revealing the brown and gray streaks that fell just below her shoulders. She wore an olive-green sweat suit and a smile that filled the entire house.

"Let me help you with that," Melissa said as she joined her aunt in the kitchen. "What are we making?"

"I thought we could make some hash browns, sausage, eggs, pancakes with whipped cream, fruit bowl…"

"Whoa, that's a lot, isn't it?" Melissa asked with a laugh.

"I just want us to have a nice family breakfast. We haven't had one since you all got here, and I've been eating alone for way too long."

Melissa smiled and hugged the woman around her shoulder. "Totally agree. We should have a nice breakfast, and I'm starving."

"Good," Aunt Elaine replied. "Now, let's get started."

She turned on the radio, and instantly the house was filled with the sounds of Christmas. They mixed the batter, beat eggs, and sliced fruit together, bumping hips as they did, and singing aloud to the songs they knew.

It was the most bliss Melissa had felt in a long time, and she bounded up the stairs with renewed vigor, her tired legs long forgotten.

"Gemma! Max! Come on down. It's time for breakfast!" she cried. She had envisioned a mini stampede when she said breakfast, but all she heard was the deafening sound of silence. "Gemma?" she asked and pushed the door in.

"Mom, I'm not up yet," Gemma moaned.

"It's half past nine," Melissa said incredulously.

"Exactly," Gemma said and pulled the covers over her head.

She didn't have better luck with Max. He was still fast asleep and barely groaned that he wasn't hungry yet. Her high hopes were once again dashed, and her shoulders sagged as she returned to the kitchen.

"Seems it's just you and me again," she mumbled and sat on the stool. "I don't get it," she said as she turned to Aunt Elaine. "They used to love family dinners and to go to the park and all that. Now? They just want to stay in their rooms. Max is always moping, and Gemma's gotten secretive. What happened to my family?" Melissa asked and threw her hands in the air. "I'm nearing the end of my rope here."

"Now, now," Aunt Elaine said and walked over to her.

"You can't blame yourself for any of this. They just grew up, that's all."

"I just hate this." Melissa sighed. "Ever since Peter left, nothing's been the same. I could see they were just keeping up pretenses. We all were. Now, I bet Gemma can't wait to get out of here."

"Don't be too hard on yourself," Aunt Elaine replied with compassion in her voice. "Sometimes, family just isn't all it's cracked up to be."

Melissa was expecting more words of wisdom and comfort— not disdain. "What?"

Aunt Elaine shrugged. "Just saying. We all think family is supposed to have your back, and we expect them to. They don't always live up to that. Sometimes, all you get is a big pile of nothing but deceit."

Melissa narrowed her eyes at the woman. "What are you talking about?"

"Nothing." She waved off Melissa and got up.

"Nothing?" Melissa asked and got up too. "You weren't talking about me, were you? That was about you and mom. What happened between you two?"

"Nothing!" Aunt Elaine snapped. "Just leave it be."

"How can I? You and Mom haven't spoken in years, and as grown as I am, no one will tell me what happened. It can't be that you're afraid of damaging me. I can take it."

"Trust me," Aunt Elaine said and slid a plate onto the counter. "Some things should just be left alone."

"I don't believe it. Mom won't say, and you won't either."

"And there you have it," Aunt Elaine advised. "If she doesn't want to say, then who am I to? Now, are we really going to let these eggs get cold?"

Melissa knew it was a waste of time, but she could see that it was something that ate at Aunt Elaine every time she mentioned it. She decided she'd let it go. There was no use in following up. She wasn't going to get a word out of either of them, but it only heightened her already existing curiosity. What could have been so bad that separated the two sisters all those years?

They both sat in silence, eating what should have been a pleasant breakfast as if it was nothing but wet cardboard. The sullen looks on their faces reflected their inner torment, and the delicious breakfast felt like a chore.

"Okay, enough of this doom and gloom," Aunt Elaine said when they were done. "I'm going to get them children, and we're going to do something fun."

"Be my guest," Melissa told her. "I'll wash up."

Melissa was blown away when, about a half hour later, both children came down the stairs, dressed and ready to go. She almost choked on the orange juice she'd just sipped. "How did you...?" She couldn't even finish the question.

"I guess they were bored after all," Aunt Elaine said as she came down behind them.

"So, I heard there was an ice-skating rink," Max said. "Doesn't sound half bad."

"What? We said that day one," Melissa exclaimed in surprise.

"Must have missed that," Max said and veered toward the kitchen.

"You need to get ready," Aunt Elaine told Melissa, who didn't need a second prompting. She quickly washed up and joined the "happy" troopers as they piled into her car, and they headed for the rink.

They seemed in better spirits when they got to the

venue and saw all the other kids there. In fact, they were having a Christmas treat and handing out cookies and hot cocoa. A Santa Claus was sitting just inside the entrance handing out toys to toddlers and those young at heart.

Several teens were milling around, and Max and Gemma lightened up a little bit more. They rented the skates, and soon enough, they were slipping and sliding over the ice. But not Aunt Elaine— she took up her position by the seating area so she could watch.

"I don't know what I was thinking," Melissa groaned as she tried to remain on her feet. Her arms were stretched out wide, and she slid from left to right, much to Max's amusement.

She managed to maintain her balance, but she quit soon after and let the kids enjoy themselves. Gemma soon huddled with two other girls who introduced themselves to her, but Max was a lot like her— he didn't make friends that easily. He did his own thing, but for the moment, she was happy.

They'd finally come out of the house, but she wondered what things would be like after Christmas. If she was going to stay in Yuletide Creek, they'd have to go to school. Max had to, anyway. Gemma would be gone by spring, and Melissa wasn't looking forward to it at all.

"They're going to be just fine," Aunt Elaine said as she suddenly appeared next to Melissa. "They just need to get situated, is all."

"I guess." Melissa sighed. "Sometimes, I think I'm not doing right by them."

"Don't say that!" Aunt Elaine said emphatically. "You have done the best you can with those kids. It's that no-good father of theirs that's the problem, so don't you go blaming yourself. All they need is a little time to adjust, and they'll be as right as rain."

"I know," Melissa said as she watched Gemma laughing with the girls.

"Would either of you ladies like some hot cocoa?" a girl dressed like an elf in a green skirt and red-and-white striped shirt asked as she rolled up to them. She was holding a tray with several steaming cups on them. "We're giving them away. You can take a candy cane and some cookies too." She grinned as she lowered the tray.

"Don't mind if I do." Aunt Elaine smiled at the girl. "Thank you, sweetie."

"No problem, Miss Elaine." She smiled back.

"I'll take a couple of those," Melissa said and picked up a cup and a cookie. "Thanks."

"No prob," the girl beamed and skated off to offer treats to the other guests.

Melissa still carried that hole in her heart from when Peter left, but somehow, she knew everything was going to be alright.

If only for Christmas!

Chapter Eight

The children were in much better spirits after visiting the skating rink. They were a lot chattier and even ventured out of their rooms more often to sit with the rest of the family.

"Mom, this tree doesn't look so bad after all," Gemma replied.

Melissa rolled her eyes at her. "Yeah, no thanks to you."

"You know I don't like all of this decorating stuff, but once it's done..."

"You get to enjoy the fruits of my labor," Melissa finished for her.

"What's for breakfast?" Max wanted to know.

"Typical," Gemma replied and rolled her eyes. "Do you ever do anything besides eat and play games?"

"Yeah," he fired back. "I watch you griping over other people's lives on IG because that's so much better."

"Okay, knock it off, the two of you," Melissa intervened. "Max, Aunt Elaine is making breakfast."

"And speaking of," Aunt Elaine said as she came into the room. "Later today, the Aldermans are having a tree gallery thing."

"A what?" Gemma scrunched up her face and asked. She was sitting at the edge of the sofa with her leg tucked under her.

"A gallery of trees," Aunt Elaine said and wiped her hand through the air as if she was painting a rainbow.

"A what!" Gemma asked again, and Max started laughing.

Aunt Elaine shook her head. "Various different people decorate trees using themes, so like last year, someone had a tree that was all ribbons. Someone else made one look like The Little Mermaid, so all the ornaments were characters from the show."

"That sounds cool." Melissa smiled and turned to the kids. "How about it? I think it will be interesting, if nothing else."

Max shrugged. "I guess."

"Yeah, what else am I going to do?" Gemma asked.

"Great," Melissa replied as excitement seeped into her. She was grateful that her children were finally warming up to being in Yuletide Creek.

"So, we're just going to look at trees?" Max asked.

"Don't make it sound like that." Aunt Elaine laughed. "They've been doing it for years, and every year it just gets bigger."

"I bet," Melissa replied. "What time does it start?"

"We can go around two," Aunt Elaine responded and walked back to the kitchen. "Until then, I have some pumpkin pie and hot cocoa for anyone interested."

"Count me in," Max said and instantly walked off.

The thought of pumpkin pie made Melissa salivate, and she raced to Max to get the first slice. He beat her to it and stuck his tongue out at her as he gloated.

"I'll get you next time," she warned him.

They hung around the house, playing cards and lazing until it was time for them to leave. The car ride to the Aldermans was a short one, but the gushing and gawking that came from Gemma was noticeable, and Aunt Elaine chuckled at it.

"I was wondering how big this house would have to be to accommodate so many Christmas trees," Gemma said as she got out of the car. "But this isn't a house at all."

"Can we just go look and go?" Max asked in an uninterested way.

"You can't tell me that this isn't cool," Gemma said forcefully. "You only see these things in the movies."

"Yep," Melissa agreed.

They all got out of the car and stood facing the large mansion set on the hill. The long driveway leading to it was lightly covered in snow, and lights adorned the path all the way to the porch. Reindeers pranced on the lawn in a glorious display of lights, and a large tree, laden with colorful ornaments right next to a life-sized Santa Claus with glowing cheeks was enough to make everyone swoon with delight.

"Hello," Yvette Alderman greeted them as they came to the door. She was dressed in all white, with bright red lipstick, a stark contrast to her pristine appearance.

"Thank you," Aunt Elaine said, and the others nodded their agreement.

"This is amazing," Melissa said as they entered the house.

"Uh-huh," Aunt Elaine muttered right before she wandered over to Melissa's right. Melissa assumed she was on her own since the children did just the same—they all went their separate ways to check out the trees that interested them. Max wandered over to one that looked like it belonged in Darth Vader's home.

Melissa was curious about the upside-down tree, but there were so many different ones that her head was spinning in no time. Children laughed and played as they darted from one tree to the next, and there were several tables in strategic positions laden with cookies, candy canes, and other Christmas treats. The smell of hot cocoa, cinnamon and spices was in the air, and Melissa followed her nose to the dining area, where several people were already gathered and waiting for their foamy treats.

"That one was done by a designer," Melissa overheard someone say behind her.

She didn't mean to eavesdrop, but she was curious as to which, so she turned so she could see as well. The woman noticed her and smiled, so she took the liberty of joining the conversation.

"I didn't mean to overhear, but I'm new here, and I found that very interesting," she said to the raven-haired woman. She wore a heavy coat with fur trimmings and an off-white scarf.

"Oh, yes," she replied and took Melissa's hand. It seemed she was the type who loved demonstrating their knowledge, but at that moment, Melissa didn't mind. "There it is," she said and showed her a tree that was more like a topiary. It was shaped like a perfume bottle and had gold and silver trinkets on it.

"Wow!" Melissa gushed. "That's nice."

"Uh-huh," the woman replied and pulled her off to

the other room. "Now look at that one," she said and pointed to another that had colorful pieces of fabric draped around a black tree. "Another designer did that. Some of them don't even look like Christmas trees if you ask me," she whispered as she pulled Melissa closer, "but they're great display pieces."

"I agree," Melissa replied.

"Oh, excuse me," the woman said and let go of her arm. "I have to go say hi to Charlotte," she said and floated off.

Melissa smiled as she watched her. She looked like a real socialite, and in Yuletide Creek, she seemed very much out of place in a room packed with simpler folk. With nothing else to do, Melissa returned to the hot cocoa station and got her cup. She stood by the main gallery area, glancing around, spotting her children with a group of teens and her aunt with company. She was the only one who seemed to be alone, so she leaned against the wall, humming to the sounds of *Have a Holly Jolly Christmas*.

She gazed around the room, and she sputtered on the cocoa when she spotted Ian. She hadn't seen him since he'd brought the tree to the house, and she hadn't really thought about him since. But there he was, and the sight of him made her heart race. She looked away, forcing herself not to pay too much attention to him, but that was even more difficult than she'd anticipated.

He was talking with a couple and another woman, and his face was lit up like the beautiful displays in the room. She admired his rugged features and the way he made a simple pair of jeans, a red and black plaid shirt, and black boots look like the sexiest thing in the world. His hair was dotted with streaks of gray and was swept back. She knew he was somewhat of a looker, but she'd never really paid much attention before then.

She contemplated going over to say hi, just so she could have some company of her own. But then she remembered their awkward exchange when they'd first met, so she decided against it. She pushed off the wall and walked out to the porch. Maybe it would be better for her to just avoid him.

She was about to climb down the steps when she felt a hand on her shoulder. She turned and almost fainted.

"Look who I ran into," Aunt Elaine gushed as she indicated Ian, who was standing behind her and grinning.

"Oh, hi," Melissa said and cleared her throat. "I didn't know you were coming."

"I was just telling him what a wonderful tree he gave us," Aunt Elaine continued. "He's really such a decent man. Any woman would be lucky to have him."

Melissa wanted to sink into the flooring. "I bet," she said weakly. She couldn't believe her aunt was openly playing cupid with her feelings.

"I bet you two have a lot to talk about," Aunt Elaine replied.

Melissa couldn't feel more embarrassed, and she could feel the blush rising on her cheeks. Ian was amused, and he chuckled. "Up to your old tricks, are you?"

"She has a reputation, huh?" Melissa laughed.

Aunt Elaine beamed. "I think I need a refill," she said and backed away.

"I don't believe her." Melissa gawked as she watched the woman hurry off. "I feel like I'm sixteen again." She kept looking at her aunt in disbelief, not wanting to turn to Ian. She didn't have a clue what to say to him, especially after that.

"So, how have you been?" he asked, forcing her to make the decision to look.

"Oh, you know." She smiled.

"Can't you take a hint, mister?" Max cried, appearing from what seemed like out of the blue. Melissa hadn't seen him since they arrived. "She said no. Just get lost!"

"Max!" Melissa said in disbelief. "Watch your mouth."

"But it's true. He keeps showing up and..."

He didn't get to finish. She took him by the arm and pulled him away. "What's the matter with you?"

"Nothing's wrong with me, but he seriously needs to know when to shove off," Max said loudly.

Some of the guests turned and started watching, and Melissa blushed bright red with embarrassment. "Max, Ian and I already talked about that, and that's not the way I taught you to speak to grown-ups."

"Well, you do it!" he told her.

That stopped her dead in her tracks. "You're right." She sighed and wiped her hand down her face. "I didn't set such a good example when I was mean to him, but that's exactly why I apologized to him. He was just being kind. Not because I lost my temper means it's the right thing to do," she finished.

Max sulked and kicked at the light snow on the ground. When Melissa looked around, some of the other guests had started walking away. There was nothing to see after all. She checked the porch in search of Ian, but he wasn't there. He'd gone back inside, but she didn't want to follow him.

"Can we just go?" Max asked in an irritated voice.

"I'd say we've outworn our welcome," Melissa agreed as she took her phone and texted Gemma.

But the embarrassment didn't wear off that easily. She brought it home with her. Ian had been such a decent man, and both she and her child had been rude to him. She wasn't sure all the treats in the world could make up for it again.

But she was determined to try.

Chapter Nine

"What happened yesterday?" Aunt Elaine asked Melissa as she joined her on the sofa.

Melissa was snuggled up with her Christmas-themed throw, watching *Home Alone* 2. "Max," was all Melissa said.

"What do you mean?" Aunt Elaine asked with worry in her eyes. "I know you seemed pretty upset when we left, but some others were already leaving, so it was fine with me."

"It's just that," Melissa began and then let out an exasperated sigh. "He got mad at Ian and did exactly what he saw me do. He thought he was bothering me, and he was rude to him."

"Oh dear." Aunt Elaine sighed. "How'd he take it?"

"He didn't say anything. But then, I didn't stick around to find out either," she said as shame filled her. "I must look so horrible to him."

"Yeah, that wasn't the best thing to do," Aunt Elaine agreed. "So, what are we going to bake this time?"

"Huh?" Melissa asked, not catching on right away to what her aunt was saying.

"Well, I assume you're going to bring Max to the tree lot to apologize to the man and bring him a peace offering again."

Melissa groaned and covered her face with her hands. "I wouldn't take another batch from me," she said. "This is just awful."

"You need to stop beating yourself up and go and see that man," Aunt Elaine replied and got up. "I think a pumpkin pie and some gingerbread cookies ought to do it."

Melissa scrunched up her face. "Oh boy. Let me go get Max. He needs to play his role right now. This is his apology. Not mine."

"That's right," Aunt Elaine said as they got to the kitchen. "I'll get the bowls."

"Max!" Melissa called when she got to his door.

He was lying on his back and tossing a football in the air and catching it. "Mom?" he replied, in question form, like he was mocking her.

"So, we're going down to the tree lot to see Ian," she began and walked into the room.

Max stopped tossing the ball and glanced over at her. "What for?"

"Because you, young man, owe him an apology. I had to do it, and now you have to as well," she told him.

"Mom!" he grumbled and sat up. "Come on."

"Yep. You were rude, and he didn't deserve it. Now we have to bake him a pie to say sorry."

Max sighed. "Can't you just go without me?"

"No," Melissa told him. "*You* were rude, so *you* have

to go and apologize to him, and we're baking him something, so you need to help with that too."

Max moaned, and his shoulders sagged as he thudded behind his mother as if he suddenly weighed twice his usual size.

Aunt Elaine was already mixing the sugar and butter and already had the dry ingredients on the counter. "You can combine those," she said to her as she chin-nodded at them.

"Okay," Melissa replied. "Max, you can put the baking sheets back where they belong, please."

"Don't think you're getting away, young man." Aunt Elaine grinned.

Max sulked as he dragged himself over to the tins, but it wasn't long before he started paying keen interest to the mixing bowl after Aunt Elaine had added all the ingredients.

"Can I mix that?" he volunteered.

"Be my guest," Aunt Elaine told him and took two steps backward.

Max started mixing the ingredients shortly before he slapped a portion onto his palm. "Hey!" Aunt Elaine laughed and hip-bumped him aside. "We need all of that for what you did."

Max grinned as he licked the batter from his palm. "Do we have to give him the whole pie?"

Melissa chuckled. "I'm sure there will be extra."

And there was. Max was overjoyed to know there would be extra pumpkin pie, and he looked forward to the stove going off. But he still had to wait for them to cool, and then after they got back from the tree lot.

Melissa spotted Ian immediately as they entered the tree

lot. He was standing at the back, pruning one of the trees. She figured he'd chase her off his property. He had every right to. Instead, he stopped clipping and smiled at her.

"Hey, what brings you by?" he asked and walked over to them.

Melissa cleared her throat and turned to Max. "Do you have something you need to say?"

"Sorry I was rude," Max mumbled.

"Speak up," Melissa scolded him. "I know you can talk louder than that."

'Sorry!" Max said louder.

"It's okay, son." Ian smiled at him and patted his shoulder. "I get it. If I had a mother like this, I'd defend her too."

Melissa blushed and swept her hair behind her ear.

"Ugh!" Max groaned when he realized what was happening. "Gross."

"Is that for me?" he asked and indicated the basket.

"Oh, yes," Melissa said and handed it to him. "I almost forgot about it."

"What's this?" he asked and peeped under the napkin covering. "Pumpkin pie? Gingerbread? If I'm not careful, my sweet tooth is going to decide fighting is a good idea."

Melissa snickered. "Is that so? I don't mind just making pumpkin pie normally."

"I don't mind getting them," Ian replied with a crooked grin. She was warm inside and being that close to Ian was triggering emotions in her she thought she'd locked away. She'd thought she wasn't ready for what being with someone meant, but after so many years of neglect, she found that she was closer than she'd thought.

"Oh, come on," Max grunted loudly, bringing Melissa back to the present.

"What?" she turned and asked Max.

"Nothing," he said and shook his head. "I'm going to wait over there."

She turned back to Ian after Max had gone. "What just happened?"

"Beats me," he said and scratched his head. "Let me go set this down somewhere."

"Okay," she replied as she tagged along behind him.

He walked inside the small building and returned empty-handed. "So, is this how you usually meet nice men?" he teased.

Melissa blushed and giggled. "Yeah. Did it work?"

"I don't know. Maybe you should keep going," he said and crossed his arms.

He stared at her with such intense eyes her southern region began to pulsate. The blush flooded her cheeks, and goose pimples lined up along her arm. She couldn't remember the last time a man had looked at her as if she was the only woman in the world— as if he actually saw her.

Her husband had been so busy chasing his dreams he'd barely had time to look up at her over the rim of his coffee cup. She could see that Ian was a completely different type of man.

"Would you two knock it off?" Max cried from behind Melissa. "We dropped off the pie. I said sorry. Can we just go now?"

"Max, you're going too far," Melissa scolded. "Go and wait for me by the car!" Max growled and stormed off, and she heard the car door slam fifty meters away. "What am I going to do with him?"

"He's a teenager," Ian offered. "It'll pass."

"Yeah, I hope so." Melissa sighed. "I'm sorry, but it's

just that he hasn't always been like this. He's just been so different since his dad left."

"It's fine, don't worry about it," Ian replied and motioned to her to walk with him. "Holidays are usually hard on a kid, with all the family shindigs in town and whatnot."

"I guess," Melissa replied. She hadn't thought about it in that light. She'd just been doing the best she could.

"Hey, being a boy at sixteen is really hard," Ian replied and shoved his hands into his pockets. "I remember what it was like when I was with my own friends. Max just got into town. A lot's going on. You just gotta give him some time."

"You're right," Melissa replied and wiped her hand down her face.

She could hardly believe how understanding Ian was. He was being an actual human with feelings, unlike her ex-husband, who was more like a robot. She'd been married, but she'd been carrying the weight of the family on her own. Her husband had kept himself isolated and only chipped in with the occasional tongue-lashing when his peace was disturbed.

She'd wanted desperately for him to guide Max— teach him how to be a man, so to speak. All he'd done was scold him and tell him to "chin up" and "be a man." Now that he wasn't there, she didn't even know how to explain that to him, and he didn't come to her for anything. If something was up with him, she'd be the last to know.

It would be nice for Max to have a decent male role model who didn't just stick his neck in the sand and wait for the storm to be over. Or pretend it didn't exist. Ian didn't have to be that guy, but she just wished she knew how to help him.

They were a few feet away from the car when she stopped walking. "I hope we're good." She smiled. "And even though I don't mind baking, I hope we don't have to have a conversation like this again."

He rocked on his heels and looked around before grinning at her. "It wasn't that bad," he finally said. "Besides, maybe if none of that had happened, you wouldn't have kept coming back for me to start liking you."

She couldn't stop blushing, even though she tried hard not to. "Not every day a girl hears that from a decent man." She beamed.

"So, how about it?" he asked and stared intensely at her again.

"What's with what?" Melissa asked him.

"You know, the diner in town serves up the best burgers this side of the Pacific Northwest. What do you say we grab a couple?"

Melissa swayed from side to side like a schoolgirl. "Ian Rooney, are you asking me out on a date?"

"Yes, ma'am. But only if you say yes. If you say no, then this conversation never happened."

She laughed. "I guess I could see what the big deal is about those burgers," she replied.

He chuckled, and his voice sent shivers down her spine. "It's a date then. How about tomorrow?"

"Sounds great," Melissa replied. She felt like she was going to explode. The novelty of the feelings took her by surprise— it was almost as if it was her first date ever. "So, talk to you later?"

"You got it," he said and reached out to open the car door for her.

"Thank you," she said and slipped inside. He closed the door, and she waved right before she drove off.

For a fleeting minute, she'd forgotten about the sulking Max in the back seat. She'd spent all their life thinking about nothing but them and caring for her family. She'd been a teacher and had been dealing with classroom stress and home stress for so long that she'd barely gotten a chance to put her feet up.

She didn't have any expectations of Ian, but it was nice to be noticed for once. Her face shone like a new penny as she drove home. Things weren't all bad— and she had the feeling she was on her way up. There weren't many things that could go wrong again.

Chapter Ten

Max didn't wait for Melissa to get out of the car when they got back to the house. He simply got out, slammed the door, and walked away.

Her lips parted to say something to him, but they closed again after she remembered what Ian had said. She was sure the divorce hadn't been easy for them either. Their family had gotten ripped apart, and their father had completely abandoned them.

"Max!" she called out to him when he was on the porch.

He stopped, inches away from the door, and turned robotically. She could see sorrow in his eyes, and it tore at her heartstrings. She walked quickly to him and gripped him on the shoulder. "What's going on with you?" she asked and moved her head from side to side as she tried to keep his eyes focused on hers.

"Nothing," he replied. "I just want to go back inside."

"Sweetie, you know if you want to talk, you can always come to me, right?" she asked.

"I don't want to talk. I just want to be alone, okay?" he asked, but the sorrow in his eyes never abated.

She knew it was a wasted effort trying to force him to cough up whatever was on his mind, but she had a pretty good idea. Family just didn't mean the same thing anymore, and she was sure he wasn't gung-ho on the whole hooking up with Ian thing.

"Okay," she said and let him go.

He turned and walked into the house, and she followed him. Aunt Elaine stuck her head around the archway wall by the kitchen.

"Auntie, why are you always in the kitchen?" Melissa asked as she walked around to the island and sat down.

"We gotta eat, right?" She winked.

"I can cook too," Melissa told her.

"Bah!" Aunt Elaine said and waved her off. "No worries. I love cooking, and it's been a while since I've had anyone to cook for but myself."

"Alright," Melissa conceded.

"So, how was it?" she asked Melissa.

"I don't know," Melissa replied in defeat. "I don't know what I'm doing wrong. I've tried to do right by the kids. I've tried to keep them together, be there for them, providing anything they needed. They still feel as far away from me as the east is from the west. I can't get through to them. All they want to do is stay locked in their rooms. And Gemma, she's keeping secrets from me. I'm losing them, Auntie," she said as despair gripped her in the bosom.

Her heart started racing as she considered the implications.

"Oh, don't do that," Aunt Elaine said as she paused in the middle of rubbing spices over the roast. "You have done a very good job with those kids. I could tell you a lot worse things they could be doing than keeping secrets and staying locked away in their rooms. So Max acts out sometimes. It's normal for teens," she said and walked over to Melissa. She leaned against the counter in front of her. "These kids are resilient. Just give them some time. All of this is still fresh for them."

"Funny, that's the same thing Ian said," Melissa said and let out a long sigh.

"Oh." Aunt Elaine grinned and wagged her brows. "Is that so? Smart man."

"Don't even go there," Melissa warned, even though her mind was always at the very place she was warning against.

"What? I didn't say anything," Aunt Elaine said innocently and returned to the roast.

"You didn't have to," Melissa replied and got up to pour a glass of water. "I can read it in your eyes."

"You're only seeing what you want to see," she teased. "But I am curious. How did it go with him?"

"How did what go? I went, he took it, and that was that," Melissa replied.

Aunt Elaine's hands stopped moving, and she pointed the wooden spoon at Melissa. "You expect me to believe that? I saw the way you two were looking at each other at the tree gallery. I can see the sparkles in them big old eyes now."

Melissa chuckled. "What sparkle?"

She would be the last person to admit to feelings she was so quick to deny. Melissa could feel the first signs of butterflies fluttering in her stomach at the thought of Ian. But she knew she couldn't focus on love when she had so much to worry about.

"Look," Aunt Elaine said and cocked her head to the side. "No one's asking you to run off and get hitched to anybody, but you can't spend the rest of your life at this pity party either."

"What pity party?" Melissa asked.

"That one," Aunt Elaine said and wiggled her hand at her. "The one where you sit around and mope over the fact that Peter walked out and that it's just you, and the kids are what matter. Don't get me wrong, they matter. A lot. But you can't live for just that. There's also you. Sooner or later, those kids are going to leave to live their own lives, and that will leave just you and a heart full of sorrow. Take it from me. Don't get too tied down to one idea. You've got to keep your options open."

Melissa scrunched up her face. "Take it from you?" she asked. "Aunt Elaine, you never had kids. What would you know about what an empty nest feels like? And keeping options open? You've been living like this since I've known you."

"Circumstances, my dear," she said and pulled her eyes away.

Melissa could see the sadness in her eyes as she tried to hide it, and she knew there must be a story behind why she'd been alone all those years. "Auntie, why didn't you get married at all? Or have children?"

Aunt Elaine clenched her jaw and placed the roast in the oven before she pulled off her mitts and turned to Melissa. "I was supposed to get married. A long time ago," she said with a half smile. Her eyes grew nostalgic, and a smile lit her face. "I was in love once with the most beautiful man there was. He was kind, loving, and everything I wanted in a husband. We were going to get married. We had our lives all worked out. I could see the picket fence, yard full of children and grandchildren, and me and him sitting on the porch watching sunsets."

"Aww," Melissa crooned. "So, what happened?"

"Another woman happened." She sighed.

"What? So, he just walked out?"

Aunt Elaine shook her head. "No, it wasn't as simple as him just walking out. I don't even think he really realized what was happening. She came to town, and I guess she spotted him and wanted him for herself and screwed me and what I wanted. She sank her paws into him, and soon enough, she got knocked up. Next thing I know, they're married, and I was left standing wondering what just happened."

Melissa's eyes popped. "What?"

"Yep," Aunt Elaine replied sadly and sat on the stool next to Melissa. "I lost my husband and everything we had planned."

"Why didn't he come back for you, though?" Melissa wanted to know.

"Child, back then, if you get someone knocked up, you better marry them, or the poor woman and child would live a hard life. He just did what he had to do. Probably wasn't happy about it. They only had one child. But he stayed with her, and I remained alone. But I never stopped loving him."

"I can imagine," Melissa said sadly as she slipped her arm around her aunt.

She turned to her. "That's why you've always been like a daughter to me. I ain't got nothing else."

"But Aunt Elaine, you could have married someone else. I'm sure you had many suitors."

"Bah!" she said and scrunched up her face. "I was too in love with him to give anyone else a real chance. I convinced myself I wouldn't be happy again, and I never was. That's why I don't want you to make the same mistake I did."

"But I'm not doing that," Melissa replied. "I just need a little time."

"Do you think I just watched him walk away and told myself that I'd never be happy again? I tried to love again. I really did. But I couldn't. And then, I realized it would never happen again, so I stopped trying. Men have come and gone over the years, but none were able to make me forget about him."

"I feel awful," Melissa replied. "I wish things had worked out better for you."

"Oh, don't you worry about that now," Aunt Elaine shushed her. "I just don't want you to let that weasel of a man rob you of any happiness. Ian's a good man, so if something's happening, let it."

"I don't know that something's happening, but he did ask me out to lunch tomorrow," Melissa finally admitted.

Aunt Elaine grinned. "That's great. I knew there was something there. You can't hide anything from an old woman."

"I wasn't hiding anything. It's just lunch. For now, we're just friends," Melissa told her. She hadn't even thought about it beyond that point. She didn't have the luxury of it, especially when she wasn't sure where his head was with it.

"Don't worry about it," Aunt Elaine said. "If it's to happen, it will. Just have fun. I just didn't want you to close yourself off from something that could be really good."

"I know," Melissa replied. "I just wish you could have

found someone after all this time. I had no idea you had to go through that."

"Water under the bridge," she said without looking and started retrieving items from the pantry to add to what she was preparing for dinner.

A commotion on the stairs caused them both to stop and look. Gemma flew into the kitchen, almost slamming into the island, her eyes peeled and her face stricken with panic.

Melissa instantly got up, thinking something was wrong with her. "Gemma, what's wrong?"

She shook her head as if she was coming out from under a spell. "Can I use your phone?"

"My phone? Why? Child, you scared me," Melissa replied and sat back down with relief.

"Sorry, but can I use your phone?"

"What for? You have a phone. Use yours," Melissa told her.

"Mine's not working, and I want to do something urgently," she said and danced from one foot to the other as if she desperately needed to use the bathroom. "Please, Mom."

Melissa studied her face and then picked up her phone. She tried to unlock it, and Gemma rushed to stand right behind her so she could see the screen. "Hey, why are you crowding me?"

"I just really want to use it now," Gemma replied.

Melissa could see the panic all over her face. "Is something wrong?"

"No. I just have to submit something for class that's due in an hour," Gemma told her.

"Okay," Melissa said and held out the phone. Gemma

grabbed it, but Melissa held on to the other end. Gemma's face contorted with confusion. "I have one condition."

"Mom, seriously?" Gemma wailed.

"Yes. If I let you use my phone, you have to dress up with the rest of us on Christmas."

Gemma's brows furrowed. "Dress up?"

"Yep. We're all going to wear Christmas onesies," Melissa beamed, and Aunt Elaine chuckled in the background.

Gemma stared at her incredulously for a couple of seconds, her face frozen as she contemplated her options. "Okay, fine. Whatever. Just give me the phone."

Melissa laughed and let it go. "Remember you agreed to that, and I have a witness!" she shouted after the fleeing Gemma. Then she turned to Aunt Elaine. "I swear, I worry about that child sometimes."

Aunt Elaine laughed again. "That's what parents do, my child."

"But I am serious about the Christmas onesies. And that includes you, too, Auntie. You get to wear a onesie too."

"Starting a new tradition?" she asked. "I take it from Gemma's expression that isn't something you always did before."

"No," Melissa said. "I just want to create some tradition we can all look forward to and get into."

"It's a good idea, and I'm always up for doing things with family," she replied.

"Me too," Melissa said. "Christmas over the last couple of years has been a pain, what with the separation and then the divorce. I totally get why they aren't into it now. They're older, and it doesn't seem as important anymore. But these are traditions they need to bring into their own families."

"That's true," Aunt Elaine agreed. "Just don't push them into it, or it won't be much fun anyway. Get them involved in doing things they like, or it's a waste."

"Yeah," Melissa replied wistfully, as the years of misery flashed before her eyes. "I hope this one leaves a lasting impression."

"You and me both, honey," Aunt Elaine replied. "Now, enough of this doom and gloom. Come and help me with dinner."

"Sure thing, ma'am," Melissa said as she joined her, and as the smell of spices filled the house, her mood was immediately lifted.

Chapter Eleven

I t had been a while since Melissa had been on a date, and the prospect of going on one sent her mind into a tizzy. She stood before the mirror, holding up one outfit after another against her body as she tried to figure out what to wear.

She wasn't sure why she was even trying to impress Ian— he'd already seen the worst of her more times than she would care to admit. Yet he'd invited her to lunch. If nothing else, he was brave.

She met him at Debbie's Diner on Main Street at two, and her heart was fluttering the entire time. She'd finally settled on a pair of black leggings and a burgundy, mustard, and white color-block oversized sweater. She finished her look with ankle boots and had her hair out and bouncing against her shoulders.

Ian wore a pair of black jeans and a white printed shirt. He had on brown boots and wore a smile that made her forget she wasn't supposed to think about him further than what he really was— a friend who had invited her to lunch.

"You look great," he said as he met her by the door.

"You clean up well too." She smiled at him. "I hope no one wants a tree today."

He chuckled. "I've got it covered. How about we go try out these wonders inside?"

"Don't mind if I do." Melissa grinned as Ian led the way and opened the door for her. But what they found inside was worse than they'd expected.

"Hmm," Ian mused. "Must be because of the holidays."

The diner was teeming with people, both locals and tourists alike. There was hardly anywhere to stand and definitely no tables. There were happy faces all around, chatting, laughing, and placing orders.

"I can't tell you the last time I've seen a diner this full," Melissa commented in awe as she slowly turned.

"What did I tell you about those burgers, huh?" Ian asked and wagged his brows.

Melissa laughed. "Maybe we should come back another time."

"Nonsense," Ian replied dismissively. "We can get it to go."

"Go where?" Melissa wanted to know.

"I know a few places." He winked as he joined the serpentine line that stretched past tables. Melissa had never tasted the food from the diner, but if she had to judge by the taste, she'd agree that it would be a treat for her taste buds.

The potent smell of beef patties on the grill, condiments, cheese, and the sugary smell of frosted drinks and soda was enough to make her stomach twist into knots. She hadn't eaten much that morning as she'd anticipated her date, and her stomach was making her pay for it.

"What do you want?" Ian asked when he finally got to the front of the line and indicated the illuminated menu board.

"Cheeseburger for me with the works and a raspberry lemonade, please," she replied.

"Good choice." He smiled. He ordered a chicken club sandwich for himself with a Coke before the two of them exited the diner. More people were still coming in as they left.

"I don't know if I should chalk it up to the limited restaurants in town or the food," Melissa joked when they got back to his truck.

"Judge it when you taste it," Ian told her. "Come on. We'll take my truck."

He opened the door and set the food down on the console before he jogged back around to the passenger side to let her in. She knew it was just a simple thing, but she was a romantic, and she appreciated the chivalry.

She felt flushed when he pulled onto the street, and she watched as the pedestrians mingled on the sidewalk, stopping to ogle the shop displays. The town Christmas tree was a beautiful centerpiece, and the Santa Claus props on the corners with ringing bells added to the joy of the season.

"This is my favorite time of the year," Melissa said as she watched.

"Yeah?" Ian glanced over and asked. "Then you chose the right time to be here."

"How come?" she asked in wonderment. She'd always known Yuletide Creek to be overly joyous during the Christmas time.

"This town has fallen off form over the years. Even this year, after Miss Ruth died, we thought the whole

Christmas House thing was going to be abandoned. But then, her daughter Ally came and took over."

"Oh, that was awfully nice of her," Melissa replied.

"Yeah," Ian said. "It was better than having Yvette Alderman hosting it."

"Wait, isn't that the lady who hosted the tree gallery thing?"

"One and only," Ian replied grudgingly. "A shameful business her husband did— swindling money from the poor taxpayers in town, and to do what? Have nicer furnishings in his home while we can't even fix the fire hydrants? Mayor Luke had such a hard time finding money to do anything. I felt sorry for the man."

"Wow," Melissa said. "I didn't know any of that."

He glanced over at her. "Sorry, I was rambling and spoiling the mood."

"No, it's okay," Melissa told him. "I wasn't bored or anything. It's good to know if I'm going to be around for a while."

"Yeah, I guess," he said as he pulled up outside a local park. There were a couple of people milling around, but not enough to warrant them having to find another place. "Here we are," he said and hopped out.

"Here we are," Melissa agreed and got out. He grabbed the paper bag, and she took the lemonade from him as he led her to one of the park benches.

"This is a whole lot better in the summer," he told her and set the food down.

"It's nice anyway." She smiled and looked around. "It's a beautiful day, and it isn't that cold. I'd say this is perfect."

"I'm glad you think so because I'm starving." He grinned.

"Me too." She laughed as they sat, and she bit into her sandwich. A couple of bites in, she stopped and stared at it as if she'd never seen one before.

"Good, right?" Ian asked with a grin so wide she could almost see the teeth at the back of his mouth.

"This is amazing, and I've had some really good ones back in Seattle," she said and bit into it again.

"Told ya." He grinned. "I don't know what the secret Is, but It works," he said.

Melissa was enjoying the warm afternoon, and she looked around at the sights. It would have been impossible not to notice it was Christmas in Yuletide Creek. She stared at Santa Claus sitting on a stool near the dried-up fountain. He was ringing a bell and sitting next to a red and white cross, which she recognized as the Salvation Army's logo.

Soon enough, Santa Claus got up and started doing a jig, much to the amusement of passersby, who dropped dollars and pennies into his bucket. Melissa got up and tossed in a few bucks herself and smiled at the man.

"That was nice of you," Ian said when she returned.

"Always willing to give to a good cause," she told him as she looked around. A couple walked by hand in hand, their faces beaming as if they were in love and could see no one else. A child ran across the other side of the park with a large German Shepherd in close pursuit, barking loudly as the boy played a game with it.

"If nothing else, a park makes for good people watching." She smiled and said aloud. Ian relaxed on the bench and crossed his arms. She noticed the faraway look in his eyes and grew curious about it. "What are you thinking about?"

He blinked rapidly before he turned to her and

smiled. "I was just thinking how I used to like people watching when I lived in the city."

She raised her brows. "The city? You're not originally from here?"

"Nah," he said and toyed with the cup in his hands like he was reliving painful memories. "Born and raised in New York City— city of all cities." He grinned as his eyes took on a faraway look.

"Wow, I wouldn't have known that," Melissa mused and turned to him so she could give him her undivided attention.

"Yeah," he said and rested his arm on the back of the bench.

"How'd you end up all the way over here? Do you have family here?"

"No. I just wanted to leave the rat race for something simpler. I felt like I was constantly getting swept away and not getting anywhere at the same time." He sighed. "Who would have thought 'simple' would have turned out to be harder?" He laughed. "Being the only tree lot owner in a small town can be pretty hard." He chuckled.

"I bet." She snickered. "So, are you glad you made that big move?"

"Uh, most days, to be honest. It isn't all good or bad. I mean, there are things that I miss, like the fact that you can never feel lonely there. It's just too busy. Some chill spots I used to have. Friends. Familiar things. I had to get used to everything again while out here. And there are dreams I wish I hadn't forfeited by coming here, but in some ways, my peace of mind was more important. There are some things the city just can't give you."

"I know what you mean." Melissa exhaled loudly. "I came here to just get away too."

"From what?" he asked.

She looked into his eyes for a couple of seconds before she spoke again. "My ex-husband, for one. The memories."

"Care to share?"

She sighed as she remembered what Peter had done. "He got busy and figured we didn't cut it anymore. He was a barely there father and husband for years, and then one day, he just up and decided that wasn't the life he wanted anymore. He did a one-eighty on his career and moved clear across the county. I waited, but he never came back. Didn't even fight for the kids, or call them, or anything. He just left us and never looked back, and I've been picking up the pieces ever since," she replied as traces of tears began to form in her eyes.

She held her head down as she tried to stave them off. She didn't want Ian to feel sorry for her, but she had no control over that.

"Your ex was an idiot!" he said bluntly.

She glanced back up, and a smile washed over her face. "You're right," she said with another deep sigh and then choked a little on the tears that refused to go away. "I'm sorry. I didn't mean to get like this and ruin lunch."

"No, that's fine," he hastened to say.

"I mean, I forgive him for what he did to me, but not for the way he abandoned the kids. He doesn't even call, and Max misses him. I know he does. Sometimes I think he doesn't say it because he doesn't want me to feel bad about it, and that's not something he should have to be worrying about."

"I agree," Ian said angrily. "That's a pretty messed up thing for a man to do to his family. No one should have to go through that with anyone, let alone children. I swear, people like that just get to me all the time," he said.

Melissa could see the anger written all over his face—how his eyes got darker and the way he clenched his jaw and tightened his fists. She couldn't believe he'd take it so personally just by hearing about her problems when he hardly knew her.

"I can tell you he doesn't know what he gave up," he said and looked her in the eyes. "So many people would want what he gave up like it was nothing."

The passion and intensity in him took her breath away. She didn't know what it felt like to be defended by anyone, let alone an almost stranger. He stared at her, and she felt incapable of ripping her eyes away from him. Her heart raced when she saw his eyes dip to her lips, and as if they had a mind of their own, they parted, inviting him closer.

It was as if they were the only people in the world who existed, and she saw his body leaning closer to her. Or was it her who was getting nearer to him? Either way, the distance between them was quickly bridged, and her eyes were almost closed, anticipating his lips on hers when a screeching sound pulled them apart as a cyclist ran into the bench they were sitting on.

"I'm so sorry," the young man replied. "My brake broke."

They saw the dangling cord on his handlebar, and Ian laughed. "It's alright, young man."

"Yeah, no harm, no foul," Melissa replied.

The young boy, who looked to be not much older than Max, nodded and shoved off on his bike, using his feet to move instead of the pedals.

But after he was gone, so was the moment. And

Melissa already regretted it. There was no doubt in her mind there was something between them worth pursuing.

"Do you want to come over for dinner?" she asked, suddenly feeling spontaneous. She could hardly believe the words that just fell from her lips. What if he thought she was being too forward?

"I'd love that," he said to her. "One more reason to leave my mountaintop fort." He chuckled.

And at that moment, she figured she'd gotten an early Christmas present.

Chapter Twelve

She could barely stop the wild beating of her heart when she got back into her car. They'd spent another hour at the park, people watching and reliving the old city lives they'd once lived. At least they had that in common, but she couldn't help wondering if his leaving was more than he'd shared.

In any case, she wasn't going to probe. He'd share if there was anything to share. But for the moment, she would bask in his attention. It felt like something new, and she was excited for the first time in a long time.

She was even more nervous because they had almost kissed. Would it be awkward for them the next time they saw each other? She wasn't sure, but she hoped it wouldn't be. Gemma was even getting into the spirit of the holidays, even if it meant her bribing her so she could loan her the phone, but she was going to take that as a win.

So far, Christmas was looking good.

She pulled into the driveway and got out of the car.

"Stay out of my room!" she heard Gemma screaming.

"What the heck?" Melissa said aloud and hurried into the house. She didn't immediately see Gemma, nor did she know who she was speaking to.

"Why did you tell me?" Max asked her.

"I didn't. You're just nosy, and that's how you know. Why can't I have a little privacy?"

"Give me back my phone," Max yelled at her. "I didn't take anything. Mom, can you tell Gemma to give me my phone back?" Max asked when he saw his mother.

He reached in for it, and Gemma pulled back, tripped over the rug, and fell backward against the Christmas tree, knocking a couple of ornaments loose.

"What's going on in here?" Melissa shouted at them. "I can't leave you two alone anymore?" She crossed her arms and glowered at them. She'd come home on a high, and instantly her bliss was wiped out by their bickering.

They had been screaming at each other before, but after she asked, they just gave each other killer stares, but no one said a word.

"I need my phone," Max said to Gemma again.

That time she complied, but neither of them said anything. Melissa crossed her arms and waited for an explanation. "Just now, all Yuletide Creek could have heard you. Do you know how disrespectful your behavior is to Aunt Elaine? You're both shouting like you're in a cage fight!"

She waited, but neither one of them spoke up, which only triggered an already frustrated Melissa. "You know what? The two of you are the most selfish and ungrateful children. Do you know how much I've given up? How much work I've put in to make sure you both will have a nice Christmas? A stable life? To make our lives normal again?" she huffed as her chest rose and fell in rapid succession. She could feel her head swelling with rage. "Your father left, and it's just been me. Me!" she said and tapped her chest. "God knows that hurt, and we all hurt from that, but that's exactly why we should stick together. You're not children anymore, for crying out loud. I can't step outside for lunch without worrying about both of you tearing the house apart! I'm tired of this! Is it too much to ask for a little cooperation? Some sympathy? Is that too much?"

"Mom," Gemma said softly, the regret writing a story across her face.

Melissa held up her hand. She didn't even want to hear it. "The decorations that you were so unwilling to help with? The ones I worked my butt off to get on that tree so the house could look decent for the holidays? They're on the floor! This isn't even our house, and you're trashing it over some petty feud."

She stopped talking and collapsed onto the sofa with her face buried in her hands. She didn't know what else to do or how much she had left to give. She'd gone through a lot, and it seemed as if no one even stopped to think about how she felt or what she was going through.

So far, the only ones who really cared was Aunt Elaine and Ian. She wasn't sure she could even be with anyone when her life was in such disarray. She couldn't keep her children from killing each other. Lately, it just felt as if she could do nothing right.

"What's going on down here?" Aunt Elaine asked as she tightened her bathrobe and padded into the living room. "I heard all this yelling, but I was in the shower."

Melissa removed her face from her hands. "Gemma and Max were at it again." She sighed.

"Oh," Aunt Elaine exclaimed when she saw the

broken ornaments on the floor. She gave the children a disapproving look. "That wasn't so nice, was it?" she asked them. "You both need to clean that up and get on up to your rooms," she said softly yet firmly.

"Yes, ma'am," Gemma replied with a sigh. She returned with a dustpan and broom, and Max dumped the larger broken pieces into the trash can while Gemma swept the fragments into the dustpan. They hung their heads when they were done and scurried off to their rooms.

Melissa was weary, and it was beginning to show. "What's wrong, dear?" Aunt Elaine asked as she sat next to her. "I heard some of what you had to say."

"It's just been an emotional day," Melissa said as she choked back the tears. "I've done everything for those children. I gave up everything for them because that's my job," she said. "But it's getting to me now, Auntie. I'm tired. I can't get a break, and they're not babies anymore. All of this has been so hard for me, losing the security I've had for years. Having to move out of the family home. Coming here. It's all been a lot in a very short space of time."

"It's a lot for all of you," Aunt Elaine echoed. "But you can't let it get the better of you. You can only do the best you can, and you're doing a good job, but even the best of us cave in impossible situations. You're only human. Not a machine. You should do what I do some-times," she said and chortled.

"What?" Melissa asked curiously.

"I pretend I was alone on this earth, and I don't have to do anything. Not that minute anyway."

"What do you mean?" Melissa pressed and shifted her body so she could see her.

"Like, I leave the dishes in the sink, or I didn't do the laundry, or I didn't clean the floor until I wanted to. Sometimes you just have to take a break despite what's going on. Maybe that's the best time to do it and get a breather so you can reassess."

"Perhaps," Melissa said and fell back onto the sofa.

The doorbell rang, and Aunt Elaine looked over at Melissa. "Wonder who that is." Melissa was so out of it that she'd forgotten that she'd invited Ian over for dinner. "It's for you, dear." Aunt Elaine stepped back with a wide grin and held the door open.

"Me?" Melissa asked as she got up. It wasn't until she saw his face that she remembered her earlier invitation. "Ian. Oh my god, I totally forgot," she told him.

He narrowed his eyes. "You just asked me about two hours ago, remember?"

"I know," she said and wiped her hand down her face. "It's just that I came home, and my children were fighting and..." she stopped before she started rambling. "I'm sorry, Ian, but now isn't a very good time at all. I'm not in the mood for company and..." she said and threw her arms in the air. "This was all just a big mistake. I don't think it's going to work out for us."

Ian stood on the porch with a confused look. "You're serious?" he asked.

Melissa didn't even know how to answer that. She didn't know what she wanted or what to think. All she knew was that she wasn't in the right headspace for company or any male company whatsoever, and she didn't want to string him along if it was never going to amount to anything between them.

"Yeah," she said weakly and stared at the floor. "I'm really sorry."

"Okay," he said as he stepped back, and the disappointment in his eyes cut to her core. But she'd already said the words. There was no going back. "I guess I'll... talk to you...later," he said between pausing as if he was trying to find the words to say. It was pretty clear he didn't understand what was going on.

How could he? She didn't even understand herself. "I guess," she answered and watched as his shoulders fell on his way to his truck. He didn't look back once, and for a fleeting moment, she thought she'd done the right thing. It wouldn't have worked out anyway.

She stepped back and gently closed the door after his truck pulled away. It was then that she saw Aunt Elaine standing with her arms crossed, wearing the deepest frown Melissa had ever seen on the woman.

Chapter Thirteen

"What's the matter with you?" she asked a shocked Melissa.

"Excuse me?" Melissa asked and narrowed her eyes. "What did I do?"

"What was that?" she asked and indicated the door.

Melissa groaned. "It was nothing, okay?"

"Doesn't sound like nothing," Aunt Elaine replied and walked after Melissa, who returned to her position on the sofa. "Did you ask him over? What happened at lunch today?"

"Nothing happened, Auntie," Melissa told her in a defeated tone. "Lunch was okay. We went to the park and talked. I asked him over for dinner," she said, pinching between her eyes as she said it.

"And you call that nothing?" Aunt Elaine asked in a disappointed voice. "You invited him over for what? Dinner? And then blew him off because you weren't in a good mood?"

"It's not like that," Melissa replied defensively.

"Well then, enlighten me," the woman said and

folded her hands in her lap. "I'm dying to hear what this is about."

Melissa had known her Aunt Elaine ever since she knew what an aunt was. Or maybe before. She'd been a constant factor in her life ever since, and the two had talked a lot over the years. It was the first time she'd ever heard her speak so frankly or sound so disappointed.

"It wasn't a good time," Melissa replied.

"Do you even hear yourself? It wasn't a good time? So, what, you just blow people off when you're not in the mood? Is that the kind of woman you are?"

"No!" Melissa cried. "What kind of a hostess would I be if my head was wrapped up with the kids and my own misery?"

Aunt Elaine shook her head. "That's not the kind of woman I took you for. Yes, things happened that you couldn't control. Yes, you've had obstacles. Yes, your children fight and don't listen, but guess what? Welcome to the real world honey!" Aunt Elaine said matter-of-factly. "Children are known to do that. You're not the first woman who's ever experienced a divorce or had moody children, and you can't keep hiding behind them."

It was Melissa's turn to be shocked. "Hiding behind them? I'm not doing that," she replied. "I'm taking their feelings into consideration and trying to give them the best that I can offer, which isn't much at this time."

"That's a load of bull if I ever heard one," Aunt Elaine retorted. "You're their mother! That's a lot. Why do you think so little of yourself? When did you get to be like this?"

"When Peter walked out and left me with all of this, and I don't have a clue how to handle it," Melissa said and got up, the tears almost blinding her.

"And I get that, honey." Aunt Elaine turned to follow her with her eyes. "Believe me, I do. I know more than most what it feels like to be abandoned by the man you love most in the world."

"At least you didn't have any kids to worry about," Melissa said and instantly regretted her words when she turned and saw the sadness in her aunt's eyes. "Aunt Elaine, I'm sorry. I didn't mean to say that."

Aunt Elaine sucked in a deep breath. "I see you're in the business of self-sabotage. At least what happened to me wasn't of my own doing."

"But I'm not sabotaging myself," Melissa replied defensively. "How am I doing that? What did I do for Peter to leave, huh?"

"I'm not talking about that worthless man," Aunt Elaine spat.

"Then what? Haven't you been paying attention to me since I got here? I've done everything I can to keep the thing on track. It's everything and everyone that's trying to sabotage me. I came home from lunch in such high spirits, and what did I come home to? My children wrecking the living room over something I still don't know!"

"Are you kidding me?" Aunt Elaine asked incredulously, her brows knitted and her eyes flashing with fire. "I've paid attention to you, alright, and you know what I've seen? You, running around here like a chicken without a head, focusing on all the things that don't matter."

"Like what?" Melissa asked in a hurt voice.

"Like getting a Christmas tree, and decorating the house, and going to events," Aunt Elaine pointed out.

"And that's not important?" Melissa asked with dismay.

"What's more important is spending time with your family," she told her.

"I've been trying to do that," Melissa wailed.

"No, you haven't," Aunt Elaine corrected her. "You don't need a tree to have Christmas. You should be focusing on the spirit of Christmas. Get that idea of the perfect family and the perfect Christmas out of your head and focus on the family that you do have and your present circumstances. You certainly shouldn't be turning away sensitive woodsmen who come knocking because they're interested in you because I can tell you from experience, it's no fun getting old alone."

Melissa was flustered by all of what her aunt had to tell her. She'd never been that real to her before, and certainly not since she'd been to Yuletide Creek. Her words were almost cruel, but they were necessary.

She covered her face in her hands. "Ugh, I'm making more of a mess than I thought."

"There's no need to beat yourself up either," Aunt Elaine said in a much friendlier tone. "What's done is done. What you need to do is fix what you can, and by that, I mean with the children and Ian," she said and tapped Melissa's hand.

"I doubt if Ian even wants to see me again, let alone give me another chance," she said as guilt flooded her. "I was so awful to him. Why did I tell him to go away?"

"You were foolish," Aunt Elaine said plainly.

"I know, I know," Melissa said and got up. "I made a mistake, and I'm the worst person on earth."

"Since when did you get so dramatic?" Aunt Elaine laughed. "All you have to do is go see the man and admit what a fool you were and bake him another batch of goodies."

"I don't think all the baked goods in the world will make up for what I did this time," Melissa said softly. "*He* would be the fool to forgive me again. I keep making a habit of disappointing him."

Aunt Elaine's brows furrowed. "Have you ever told him about Peter and why you came here?"

"A little," Melissa replied. "When we had lunch today."

"Well, there you have it," Aunt Elaine said excitedly.

Melissa wrinkled her brows. "Have what?"

"If you already told him about your difficulties, then he is likely to be more patient with you," she suggested. "Just go and have a talk with him, and don't go make another mess."

"I don't know," Melissa replied doubtfully. "Seems I have a knack for it. Maybe I should just spare the poor man all this drama and leave him alone."

"You need to stop talking that nonsense unless you want to end up like me," Aunt Elaine said and glared at her.

"Doesn't seem so bad from where I'm sitting," Melissa mumbled.

Aunt Elaine flashed her a warning look. "Child, don't talk about what you don't know," she said and walked to the kitchen. Melissa followed her. "Lord knows I wanted the love of a good man, but I'd closed myself off to it a long time ago. By the time those men came knocking, I was a lost cause, and I'd spent the rest of my life feeling nothing but self-pity. You don't want that. Take it from me," she said and pointed at Melissa emphatically with her wooden spoon.

Melissa laughed. "Okay. Point taken."

Aunt Elaine shook her head in disbelief and tossed

the spoon in the sink. "I'm going to wash up. Do you want to start on dinner?" She tightened her face and headed upstairs.

"Yeah," Melissa replied and dragged herself into the kitchen.

"And talk to those kids!" Aunt Elaine shouted back to her.

Melissa was completely confused after she left. She stood beside the kitchen island, propping herself up by her elbows. Even if she were going to take baked goods to Ian, she was still anxious about going to see him. She wasn't sure how he'd react after her foolish rejection of him. She wanted to kick herself for what she'd done. At the moment, it had seemed like the right thing to do, but she knew she had been wrong.

She couldn't fix it that evening, but there was one thing she could fix— her children. She turned her head and glanced at the row of stairs separating her from them. Dinner could wait. She had to find a way to reach her children. Aunt Elaine had been right— Christmas was more than just a tree, fancy ornaments, and lights.

She shoved off the island and started making her way up the stairs.

Chapter Fourteen

She stood in the hallway, looking from door to door, wondering who she should speak with first. She finally decided on Max— Gemma might prove to be more difficult.

She knocked and then opened it before he could even answer.

"I don't want to talk," he said as soon as she entered.

"I don't care," she replied and crossed her arms as she glared at the insolent boy. "You're going to have to."

He rolled over onto his stomach and growled. He knew he couldn't fight her, and he wasn't about to try.

Melissa knew she had an uphill battle in front of her, but it was one she had to face. "Do you mind telling me what's going on with you?" she asked as she walked closer to Max. He looked up at her with downcast eyes and shrugged. "That's it?" Melissa asked with disappointment. "You think I don't see the way you've been acting lately? You're either locked away in your room, or you're fighting with your sister."

"Nothing's going on, Mom," Max groaned and rolled his eyes.

"Max, I didn't raise you this way, and I know you've seen your dad and I fighting a couple of times, but fighting is always wrong," she told him. "It's never okay."

"Neither is lying!" he retorted, and his face reddened as if he was carrying anger she knew nothing about.

His outburst surprised Melissa. "Lying? What did I ever lie about?"

"Not you," he said, and then his eyes told her he didn't mean to say that. He hung his head and turned around. "Can I just go play some video games?"

"Who's lying? Gemma?" Melissa asked as her heart started beating rapidly. She tried to replay the conversations she'd had with Gemma that would have detected the lie she'd told her. Or Max. "What did she lie to you about?" She automatically thought she must have lied to Max.

"Nothing," Max replied.

"It can't be nothing." Melissa laughed nervously and sat on the bed next to him. "Clearly, it was something, and I want to know what it is."

"It's not important," Max insisted.

She had to give him his props— he was angry at his sister, to the point of the two of them almost ripping each other to shreds, yet his loyalty to her was fierce. She would admire it even more if it wasn't in complete defiance of her and what she wanted. She sighed with defeat. Melissa knew there was no way she was going to get an answer out of him. He was much like her— sensitive and loyal.

She squinted her eyes at him and cocked her head to the side as she studied his face. She still didn't know what the fight was about, but there seemed to be something else going on. "Wait, is all of this attitude and sulking all about Gemma, or is there something else?"

"I don't know what you're talking about," Max replied in an annoyed voice. "By the way, what about Ian?"

His question took her by surprise. "Ian?"

"Yeah." He shrugged. "I thought I heard him before."

It was Melissa's turn to be embarrassed. "Uh, yes, we went out for lunch, and then I invited him over for dinner. But then, I came home to the two of you fighting, and it crushed me, and he showed up, and I kinda told him it was a bad time, so he left. It was probably a bad idea anyway."

"Okay," Max replied with a hint of disappointment but noticeable. *Does he want Ian and I to be together?* She began to think that he really missed his father, and that may be troubling him more than he was letting on. "Are you and him going to be a thing?"

"I don't know," she replied with a deep sigh.

"You don't like him?" he continued.

"I do," she said as she got up and started pacing the floor like a nervous child undergoing a parental inquisition. She was about to answer him further when she came to her senses. She was the parent. She didn't have to answer to him. But she knew she also owed him more than she was giving. "Look," she said and turned to Max. Melissa walked over to him and placed her hands on his shoulders so she could look him in the eye. "I'm your mother, and it is my job to look out for you and your sister. You come first and should be my top priority, okay?"

"Yeah," Max mumbled. "Maybe if you had someone else, you'd stop trying so hard with us."

Melissa widened her eyes in shock. "Max!"

"What? It's true," he said. "You hover. A lot."

"That's only because you two don't make it easy, so now I have to micromanage. If I could trust you to not rip the place or each other apart every time I wasn't around, I wouldn't feel the need to be so hard on you."

"Well, I'm okay," Max reassured her.

"Promise you'll tell me if you aren't," she said with concern in her eyes.

"Fine," he replied. "Can I go back to...?" he asked and indicated the computer without finishing the sentence.

"Alright," she said and headed for the door.

She hadn't gotten anywhere with Max, and she didn't have any reason to believe she'd have better luck with Gemma. She was beginning to rethink approaching her in the first place when she closed the door and turned right into Gemma.

Melissa jumped and clamped her hand on her chest. "Gemma, what are you doing out here?" She stood with a clenched face and crossed arms as if she was ready to come down on her mother for something.

"Nothing," she said with tight lips and a piercing glare.

"What's the problem? I was just coming to see you."

Gemma squinted at her. "To see me? Why?" she asked curiously, and Melissa watched as her chest started rising and falling quickly.

"You seem nervous. What's wrong? Are you not feeling well?" Melissa asked and walked closer to Gemma.

She backed away. "I'm fine, Mom."

"Okay," Melissa told her. "There's still that conversation that we need to have. I just talked to Max, and I didn't like the way our conversation ended," Melissa said and crossed her arms. "I'm hoping I can put this to rest now."

Gemma pressed her palm against her forehead. "Oh my god, this isn't happening," she said as she started to pace the floor. "What did Max tell you?"

It was Melissa's turn to be confused. "What do you mean what did he tell me? Is there something I should know?"

"Wait, I thought you said Max told you something," Gemma said, her eyes betraying her confusion.

"I said our conversation didn't end like I thought it would, but now, you're making me second-guess all of that. There's something you're not telling me."

"I didn't do anything," Gemma said quickly.

"No one said you did, but by the way you're acting, I'm pretty sure you did," Melissa replied and walked over to her daughter. "What aren't you telling me?"

"Nothing," Gemma said and wheeled around as if she intended to go back to her room. "Forget it."

"Don't you walk away from me, young lady!" Melissa retorted and skipped in front of Gemma, blocking her from going back into the room. "I am talking to you. Now you're going to talk to me right now!"

Gemma was fuming as she stood outside the door. "What do you want to know?" she asked her with all the eighteen-year-old attitude she could muster.

"Just talk to me," Melissa pleaded. "I know there's something going on, and you won't tell me what it is."

"Nothing's going on, Mom," Gemma repeated.

Melissa sighed. It was like talking to a wall. Gemma was no different than Max. That was probably the one thing they had in common— they were like a fortified wall of secrets, and no amount of battering would weaken their defenses.

She'd have to get to her another way, and as she saw the fire in Gemma's eyes, the same fire she'd known when she was her age, she became subdued. What Gemma was doing didn't work when her mother had tried it on her as a teenager, and it wasn't working for Gemma either.

Melissa stepped back and held her hands up. "You know what? I was just telling Max how wrong fighting is, and I'm not going to keep doing it with you. I have a better idea."

Gemma rolled her eyes. "Let me guess. Another Christmas tradition. I already agreed to one."

Melissa smiled. "No, not that. How about you get dressed? Let's go for a walk."

Gemma stared at her as if she was speaking in Mandarin. "A walk?"

"Yeah." Melissa grinned. "Come on. "It's good for clearing your head and releasing endorphins that will put you a better mood."

"Okay, stop talking," Gemma said and flailed her arms. "I'm coming."

And Melissa laughed and walked away as Gemma disappeared inside her room.

Chapter Fifteen

Melissa doubted Gemma would come downstairs. Every couple of minutes, she peered up the stairs, expecting to see her appear at the top of the staircase. After ten minutes, the doubt began to sink in. She was walking toward the stairs when Gemma started jogging down, and Melissa's heart warmed.

"Let's just go before I change my mind," Gemma said as she hurtled past her mother as if she was shot from a canon. She was dressed in a black running suit, and her hair was caught at her nape in a ponytail. "There shouldn't be any shortage of places to walk in this town."

"Nope." Melissa smiled. She knew there would be a fifty-fifty chance of Gemma shutting down her request, but she was glad that she hadn't. "Let me tell Aunt Elaine we're heading out. Wait for me by the car."

"The car?" Gemma asked midstride. "I thought we were going walking."

"We are, but I want to go to the coast. I haven't been

there in a while, and it should be really peaceful at this time of the year."

"Oh," Gemma replied and shrugged. "Whatever."

Melissa hurried to inform Aunt Elaine that she was heading out and then joined Gemma in the car. "We used to do this when you were younger." Melissa smiled.

"I don't remember," Gemma said, unconcerned as she poured over her playlist.

"Of course, you don't," Melissa replied. "There are a lot of things you don't remember." She drove down Main Street, observing the town's festivities. There were times she forgot the season— like when she had to fight with her children. But driving through town, seeing the gay faces and children running around in the light, snow flurries that were sprinkling the air, it reminded her of a town where life was simple, when she had her family intact, and Peter hadn't started showing his true colors.

The children were younger, and they'd go to the park and roll around on the red, green, brown, and orange fall leaves. She still had the pictures of the last time they did that, and her heart grew heavy from the memory.

She cleared her throat and glanced over at the unsuspecting Gemma, who was staring through the window. She had her ear pods in, so she wasn't hearing anything. Melissa wasn't sure she even saw all the lights and ornaments outside and all the happiness and laughter that surrounded them.

Soon enough, they left the lights behind and headed onto a lonelier stretch of road. It was a scenic route, with the bare branches reaching out to each other as if they were trying to stay alive despite the winter chill. It was a breathtaking view of the Yuletide Creek's landscape— snow-capped mountains, the swirling bluish-gray sky, and the once lush green land resting for winter. The large limestone rocks made natural retaining walls, and vines crept along the surface from the ground to the top, crisscrossing each other in brown webs.

Pretty soon, the sound of waves crashing on the shore placed a smile on Melissa's face. She stopped the car about half a mile away, and they both got out.

"So, when you said walk, what you really meant was drive," Gemma said and closed the door.

"Don't tell me this isn't nice," Melissa said as she set off down the path.

"Meh," Gemma grunted and followed her.

The path, thanks to the dead plants, made an easier path for them to follow to the shore. When they stood against the pebbled path that led to the sandy beach, Melissa stopped and sat on a rock that jutted out.

"This is beautiful, isn't it?" she asked Gemma.

"I guess," she said and took a seat next to her mother. "I've never really admired the ocean before," she replied wistfully.

"You've been to the beach before," Melissa told her. "What are you talking about?"

"Yeah, to swim and play around," Gemma replied. "Not to just sit and look at it."

"Oh," Melissa said. "This has been one of my favorite things. It's amazing to me how something that looks so violent as waves beating against the cliff, splashing water all everywhere, can be so calming."

"Yeah," Gemma agreed. "I have to admit you're right this time."

"Wow," Melissa said and glanced over at her daughter.

"Yeah, I know. I must be coming down with something," Gemma mocked.

Melissa laughed, and the sound carried to the waves breaking against the reef. The wind was slowly moving across the waters and teasing the hairs at the back of their necks. It was a cool day, but one that only required a pullover, which made it perfect.

Melissa got up and inhaled the salty air, spreading her arms wide and closing her eyes. "I've missed this," she said and opened her eyes again. "Hey, I have an idea," she said and turned to Gemma.

"Uh-oh," Gemma replied. "Here it comes."

Melissa laughed. "How do you feel about collecting some souvenirs?" she asked, even as she started looking around.

"Do you mean rocks?" Gemma asked and got up.

"Or anything interesting. There's a treasure chest out there sometimes," Melissa said excitedly as she stooped. "Look! Sea glass."

"Yeah, that's cool," Gemma said and started looking around too. "Oh, a three-color shell!"

"See? Enjoying yourself already." Melissa smiled as the two set off down the beach, tripping over loose stones as they pried beneath rocks and at the water's edge for treasure. They lost track of time as they walked further down the beach, trading cool things that they found until they noticed that it had started snowing.

Gemma closed her eyes and started turning around in circles, her arms held wide and her tongue out. Melissa chuckled at her silliness, but she had missed the girl that had been silly. So many things about her family had changed when Peter had abandoned them, and it was nice to see a glimmer of that memory in her daughter.

"Maybe we can go over to that cleft," Melissa told Gemma and pointed to an overhanging rock. They trekked to it and sat on the ground, watching as the snow fell and the waves kept hammering the reef.

Melissa glanced over at Gemma, and the anxiety in her slowly began to intensify. She knew she should start the conversation, but she also didn't want to ruin the mood. It had been a long time since she and Gemma hadn't argued. She was hesitant, but that only made her more suspicious when Gemma noticed her twitching.

"What is it, Mom?" she finally asked. "You can say it."

Melissa sighed. "I was just...I was thinking about how I talked to Max earlier. When I came home, you two were fighting about something, and he told you to stop lying. Earlier, when I told him fighting wasn't okay, he said neither is lying."

Gemma groaned. "This again."

"Yes," Melissa said firmly. "I get the feeling that he is keeping something from me, and it has to do with you. Now, I know it's great that he is loyal, despite your fighting, but he shouldn't be carrying that weight. I could see how much it was eating away at him."

"I didn't give him a secret to keep," Gemma protested. "He just...overheard something."

Melissa sighed. "That's sort of the same thing. I'm guessing you warned him against telling, but it's been bugging him so much it's causing fights between you."

Gemma sighed and wiped her hand down her face. "I know," she said and removed her hand. She stared out at the water for a long time. "I don't think I did good on the college placement test."

Melissa didn't expect that, and her eyes widened in horror. "What?"

"Yeah, that's my little secret, okay?" Gemma asked and stared at her feet as she rubbed her palms together. "He heard me talking on the phone, and he threatened to tell you, and I warned him off."

"But why? I thought you really wanted to go, and you had it covered."

"Not really. It didn't feel right," Gemma turned to her mother and explained. "I know it was wrong to pressure Max into keeping this secret, but for so long, I wanted to tell you, but I knew you wouldn't listen. You were a teacher, and you wouldn't hear about it."

"I'm sorry you felt that way," Melissa replied sorrowfully.

"I just don't have my future figured out yet, and I don't want to go to college and waste my time anyway, doing something I'm not sure I'm even going to use. And I knew you couldn't possibly understand. All you've ever talked about is college and how important it is. When I realized I wouldn't be going at all, I just kept quiet."

"When did you find out?" Melissa asked, surprised that Gemma had been holding things back for longer than she'd thought.

"Not so long ago," Gemma replied and turned to her mother. "Remember that time I told you my phone wasn't working, and I needed to use yours?"

"Yeah," Melissa said tentatively, her heart rate increasing by the second.

"The school had sent an email with the results of the test, and I didn't want you to see it, so I took your phone and deleted it."

Melissa was getting more shocked by the minute. "Gemma!"

"I know it was wrong, but I wasn't ready to tell you

yet, and I didn't want you to freak out," Gemma explained.

It was a lot for Melissa to take in, but she thought Gemma was hiding something worse than what she'd revealed. She sighed with relief when she realized it wasn't that bad. "Honey, I know I can be pretty hard on you sometimes, but not knowing what you want to do at eighteen isn't the worst thing in the world."

"Really?" Gemma asked. "You don't have a problem with me not going to college?"

"It's not that big of a deal. It's your life, and only you can decide what you want to do and know when you're ready for it. I know I pushed the whole college thing because that's what I would like you to do, but you have your whole life to figure that out. You don't have to make up your mind at eighteen."

Gemma stared at her she was looking at a ghost. "Those were not the words I expected to hear."

Melissa smiled. "I remember all too well the reason your father left. He wanted to do something else with his life, and in the end, that didn't include us."

"Poor example, Mom," Gemma said and shook her head.

Melissa laughed. "I know, but it did teach me something. Don't do anything you don't want to. You can get your experiences and decide what to do when you're comfortable, but I don't want you doing anything just because I said so. And I especially don't want you going behind my back because you don't think you can talk to me, okay?"

"Okay, Mom." Gemma smiled. "I'm sorry. I guess some things have changed after all."

"Tell me about it." Melissa chuckled. "There was a

time when I thought I had my future all figured out. I wanted a husband, children, a yard with a picket fence and a golden retriever. And for a while, I thought I had that perfect life, minus the retriever, of course."

"Of course." Gemma smirked as she listened intently.

"But then, things didn't go according to plan. It started going bad long before Peter left. I just didn't think he would up and leave the way he did, so then I was left with two broken hearted children, being a single parent, and trying to hold everyone down and be a teacher at the same time. It was overwhelming, to say the least. I barely got a chance to process my emotions, so I know a little something about making big choices too soon."

"I have to say you're wowing me right now," Gemma told her. "You're amazingly cool about all of this."

"Yeah, I learned that it's not very easy to try to mold something as fluid as life exactly the way you want it, and even then, there's no guarantee about being happy in the end. You start to compare yourself with other people and wonder why they're making it, and you're not."

"You've done that?" Gemma asked.

Melissa shook her head. "A few times. I've felt like a failure a million times, but I guess it goes with the territory of being a parent."

Gemma gasped when her mother said that. "I had no idea it had been so hard for you. You mask it very well."

"I had to," Melissa told her. "I had to think about you and Max."

"Wow. But I must say, Mom, I'm glad we're having this talk. Normally you just tell me to let the grown-ups handle it."

Melissa smiled and stroked her face. "Well, I guess you're grown up now, huh?"

Gemma grinned. "Enough."

"It does feel good to be able to talk to you openly, like a friend, and not just like a mother to a daughter," Melissa said.

"It does feel good," Gemma said, and her face fell. "I just didn't understand how much you were carrying, Mom."

"Don't worry about it," Melissa told her as she felt the lump rising in her throat. "I don't need you to be sad about it."

"Too late," Gemma replied. "What Dad did. Your dreams, and then Max and I are always fighting and making things more difficult?"

Melissa smiled through the tears that were forcing their way to the front of her eyes. "You didn't know, and you were too young to understand."

"I get it now," Gemma said and placed her head on her mother's shoulders. The two remained silent for what felt like a very long time as they tried to process their grief. Suddenly, the waves crashing against the cliffside were appropriate to the turbulence inside them, and tears started rolling down Gemma's face. "I'm so sorry, Mom," she said and wiped the tears away. "I've been a crappy daughter. I just wasn't thinking about how this was hurting you."

"Hey," Melissa said and cupped Gemma's face. "You're a really good daughter, and I wouldn't have traded you for the world. I love you, my child," Melissa said and cradled her again against her bosom.

"Warts and all?" Gemma sniffled and wiped her eyes.

"Warts and all," Melissa replied as the two hugged each other in a way they never had before. They were closer than they had ever been, and all it had taken was the revelation of a secret that wasn't necessary, to begin with.

"I love you too, Mom," Gemma whispered.

"I know, sweetie," Melissa said and kissed her forehead.

They held each other and watched the rolling waves, letting nature soothe their sorrows.

"I think we should head back now," Melissa finally said. "Looks like the snow's coming down harder."

"Yeah," Gemma agreed and got up. "We should do this more often." She turned to her mother and smiled, and they clasped their fingers together and walked toward the car.

"It's a deal." Melissa smiled back.

She felt lighter than she had in years. Now, if only she could get through to Max.

Chapter Sixteen

Melissa returned home, feeling in high spirits after her talk with Gemma. For the first time in a long time, she felt as if things were finally looking up.

But that was before she walked into the living room and stared at the half-naked tree with limping ornaments that made the room look like Halloween. All that was missing was a Jack o' Lantern with jagged teeth.

Melissa groaned as she retreated to the basement. The only thing she'd done after the brawl was to have the kids clean up their mess, but she hadn't replaced any of the broken ornaments, and since she was already in a happy place, she figured it would be the perfect time to fix the tree. Besides, with the tree looking so shabby, it wasn't helping the Christmas mood.

The minute she stepped into the basement, she had second thoughts. There was a cold chill in the air, and she hugged herself as she walked around the gloomy space. She spotted the carton box in the corner with the bold, green label that read "ornaments" and shuffled over to it.

She remembered how tedious it had been the first time, and for a fleeting moment, she considered just scrapping the tree. Aunt Elaine had made a good point before about them not needing a tree to have a great Christmas, and she had been right. But still, she couldn't let go of that part of her that felt as if a tree made the season brighter.

So, she picked up the box and marched back upstairs to tackle the unwelcome task once again. All the while she took the ornaments from the box, she kept thinking about Max. She'd gotten through to Gemma, but Max would be a closed dam. He wasn't as forthcoming and would probably deny that anything was wrong with him in the first place. But he was her child, and she knew he was withdrawn.

Before they'd moved to Yuletide Creek, he was an outdoorsy kind of child— always running around with the animals or collecting insects. He was sensitive, which made him unpopular with the "all-masculine" types. Things got worse when he no longer had his father around, but Melissa had been trying to cope with her own emotional baggage that she'd just been glad they weren't crying. She should have taken that as a sign— that they didn't ask about him either.

He was going to be a tougher nut to crack because she'd always found it harder to get him to open up. His father had been good at that, and her lips tightened as she fought the bad memories that flooded her consciousness.

She fought back the tears, but by then, it was too late. She wasn't in the mood for decorating anymore. The tree would have to wait. She was about to head to the kitchen when she spotted Aunt Elaine as she stepped onto the landing.

"Hey, baby girl," Aunt Elaine replied and then sighed.

"Hey, Auntie." Melissa smiled weakly. "Is everything okay? You seem a little under the weather."

Aunt Elaine waved her off. "Don't worry about me. It's just old age, is all. You'll understand soon enough." She chuckled and hobbled toward the living room. "Oh, I see you got the ornaments out again."

"Yes, I tried to put them up again, but I wasn't feeling it. I figured I'd do something else and maybe get back to it later."

"I told you," Aunt Elaine reminded her. "You don't even need the tree."

"Something tells me I do. I know you don't like it, but it helps with the whole feeling of Christmas."

"Oh no, I didn't say I didn't like the tree. I said you didn't need one to have a good Christmas. There's a difference," she pointed out and raised her brows at Melissa.

"You know what I mean." Melissa laughed.

"Well, if you need something to do, you can start dinner. I'm not feeling up to it. There's steak or salmon if you want."

"Yeah, I don't mind," Melissa told her. "Besides, I need something to do, or I'm going to get crazy." And she meant it. The house was quiet, and everyone seemed to be in a melancholy mood. She hadn't seen Max since she returned, and she wasn't sure how to approach him again. She needed the distraction, and dinner proved an easy one.

Aunt Elaine curled up on the sofa and pulled the throw over her legs as she prepared, and Melissa retreated to the kitchen. She hoped she'd have the energy to tackle the tree later, plus they still had presents to wrap. Christmas was only a few days away, which didn't give her much time, and she didn't want to be overly busy on Christmas eve.

She was feeling a little better when she got to the kitchen. That had been one of her favorite places back in Washington, preparing meals for her family. But even that love had diminished somewhat as she'd gotten distracted with the divorce and keeping her family together.

But it was a new day, and she was determined not to make the same mistakes all over again. And she'd begin with a lovely dinner they could all enjoy. She decided that she'd make pan-seared salmon with baked potato cubes and asparagus. It wouldn't take long, but she wished Gemma would spend more time around her so that they could do more mother-daughter things. She sighed as she rubbed the spices over the salmon and placed them in the skillet.

Soon, the kitchen smelled divine, and Melissa plated four dishes and brought them to the dining table. She stood at the bottom of the stairs and called the children. They were downstairs in minutes, but the sullen looks were unmistakable. Gemma smiled weakly, but Melissa could see a hint of sadness behind her eyes. She'd tried so hard to keep things together, but she could feel herself unraveling as she imagined herself a failure. Her children weren't happy, and she wasn't sure what else she could do to remedy that.

They took their places at the table, with their heads hung, focused on the meal, as if everyone was trying to avoid each other.

"So, are we just going to sit here?" Melissa asked as she tried to stir them up.

Aunt Elaine grunted and stuffed some asparagus in her mouth. "This tastes great."

"Thank you," Melissa replied and raised her brows. That was not the discussion she was hoping to have, but when she looked around the table at the other faces, they looked like automatons. "Come on, guys," a frustrated Melissa finally said. "What's going on? Gemma? Max? We used to have so much to talk about at dinner."

"That was then," Max was the first to say.

"Yep," Gemma agreed. "I don't really have anything to say."

Melissa sighed. "Fine."

The dinner that had tasted heavenly before developed a bland taste in Melissa's mouth. Her mouth moved in slow, circular motions, but she wasn't tasting anything until soon, like everyone else, she lost her appetite. She excused herself and returned to the kitchen.

Aunt Elaine followed her. "Don't beat yourself up too much," she advised.

"How can I not?" Melissa said sadly. "Look at them. No one would believe they were my children. They're like aliens."

"Sweetheart," Aunt Elaine said and cupped her face. "All of this is still new. You must give it some time. What all of you are experiencing didn't happen overnight. You took some time getting there, and you'll take even more time getting it out of your system. It's the same for them. They'll come around. You wait and see."

"I guess," Melissa groaned.

"Now, how about we get this place cleaned up?" Aunt Elaine asked.

Melissa knew she wasn't feeling well before, so she was really going the extra mile to put a smile on her face. "Yeah, let's do that before I lose the will to do anything."

Aunt Elaine chuckled. "I'll give the rascals a little talk, see if that works."

"Thanks." Melissa smiled. She'd never turn down a helping hand when it came to her children. She was aware she couldn't do it all, and if someone else were able to get through to them, then she wasn't going to let her pride get in the way.

Max and Gemma cleared the table, but then they disappeared afterward, which Melissa knew would happen. They remained confined to their bedrooms as if they were completing jail time.

"Don't mind them," Aunt Elaine said as she started prerinsing the dishes. "But about you," she said and looked across at Melissa as she loaded the dishes into the dishwasher.

"What about me?" Melissa wanted to know and peered at her curiously.

"Have you talked to Ian yet?" she asked her pointedly and stood upright, facing her as if she was a drill sergeant.

Melissa almost felt the need to salute her. "No," she replied and quickly turned her eyes away. "I didn't get a chance to?"

"What does that mean, you didn't get a chance to? What's stopping you because I know for sure it ain't him."

"What do I say?" Melissa asked naively.

"You say that like you just stood up a boy for the high school prom," Aunt Elaine remarked. "This is a grown man, and you've embarrassed him, yourself, *and* me."

"You?" Melissa asked, shocked at her aunt's accusation.

"Yes, me!" Aunt Elaine exclaimed.

"Look, I know I messed up with him a few times, which is why I think it's best if I just say away from him," Melissa said without looking at her aunt.

The pot that Aunt Elaine was holding clattered in the sink, and when Melissa turned to see what it was about, she saw her glowering at her with her hands placed on her hips. "That's your solution?"

"I don't see what else makes sense at this point. I feel silly showing up at his shop with baked goods every time I do something wrong. And that seems to be a lot."

"Yeah, it's like you're deliberately trying to push him away," Aunt Elaine said.

"I'm not, but maybe I'm just not ready to be with someone. Every time I try to mend something with him, I start a whole other problem."

"No," Aunt Elaine told her and started the dishwasher. "You keep doing the same things over and over again, and let me tell you," she said and walked over to Melissa. "I'm the one who has to live here when you're gone, and I don't want to have the reputation of having rude relatives. Now, you better go and apologize to that man. He was just trying to be nice, and you were the one who invited him to dinner."

"I know, but I don't see how that would give you a bad reputation," Melissa countered. "No one even knows about this except for us and him."

"Doesn't matter. I don't want to have to hold my head in shame every time I have to go to the tree lot or when I pass him on the street."

"Auntie, it's not that bad," Melissa replied as her shoulders sagged. "I don't even think it's like that. I don't take him as the kind of man who gossips. He's barely in town."

"And that makes a difference? You shamed the man, and now you find excuses to make it right. Even if you don't want to be with him, he deserves more respect than that."

Melissa couldn't argue with that. She had been wrong in the way she had treated Ian when he had been nothing but kind and forgiving. The shame started to penetrate her, and she remained silent all the while she finished tidying the kitchen.

Aunt Elaine disappeared soon after, and with nothing else to do, so did Melissa. The house was dull, despite the tree, and her heart fluttered. She sat on the edge of the bed and stared at the phone like she expected it to either speak to her or call Ian on her behalf.

It had been a while since she'd had to do anything of the sort— calling a man and playing the whole dating game. She'd been married since her youth, and the awkward feeling engulfed her.

She sighed and turned the phone over and over in her trembling hands as her chest heaved as if she was carrying a great burden. Melissa knew Aunt Elaine had been right. She had to make right with Ian, and it was better if she just got it over with.

Or maybe, she could just text. She figured that might be an easier way to communicate with less awkwardness.

Ian, I'm very sorry about the way I let things happen the last time...

She began to type, but her nerves got the better of her, and like a teenager, she deleted the message and heaved an exasperated sigh.

I know I've done this a lot, but I'm really sorry for being so mean...

Another deletion. She couldn't seem to get the words out right without sounding like a sap.

Can we talk?

Delete. She sighed again and tossed the phone onto the bed before she fell backward beside it. She wiped her hand down her face. Maybe she'd call him the following day when she had better control of her emotions.

But even as she pulled her feet up under her, she knew tomorrow didn't hold the promise for better.

Chapter Seventeen

Things were awkward in the morning when Melissa woke. Her stomach was churning, and her heart was beating rapidly. She knew it was her anxiety acting up, but she also knew she couldn't let it get the better of her.

She'd figure everything out, including what she was going to do once the holidays were over.

What she didn't expect was the cheery household she ran into when she eventually made it to the living room. She'd expected to spend the day alone, again, considering everyone had been in a mood earlier, but that was not the image that greeted her.

Aunt Elaine was wrapped up, literally, in ribbons and bows, gift stickers clinging to her as she tried to navigate herself around the mess that she'd made in the living room as she attempted to wrap the presents.

"Good morning." She smiled at Melissa as she tried to detangle herself from the web of her making.

Melissa laughed. "Good morning. Need a hand?"

"Need two." Aunt Elaine chuckled. "I wanted to get this out of the way, but clearly, I'm out of practice."

"Well, I'm not," Melissa said as she joined her.

The living room finally resembled what a house before Christmas should look like. Candy canes were sticking out of the stockings over the fireplace, a few boxes of presents lay under the Christmas tree, which still needed to be finished. She'd get to it later. For the moment, there were several gift bags with gifts spilling out of them and boxes that needed wrapping.

"Okay," Melissa said as she settled into her spot on the sofa. "Where do I begin?" she said, more to herself than to the room.

"Anywhere you like," Aunt Elaine said as she inadvertently taped her finger to the box. "Oh, come on."

Melissa laughed. "Not as easy as it seems, is it?"

"That's why I stick to gift bags and tissue paper." She chuckled. "And even then, I get the gift bags with the tissue paper already in it or the gift boxes that already look wrapped."

Melissa giggled out loud. "It's not that bad. It gets easier with practice," she said.

"I didn't get much of that," Aunt Elaine said. "Besides the twice-yearly gifts I used to send over the years before Gemma and Max were born."

"I remember." Melissa smiled. "If there was one gift I could count on, it was yours. Without fail," Melissa said as she remembered her aunt with fondness.

"I couldn't disappoint my baby girl." Aunt Elaine grinned, and her eyes twinkled when she did.

Melissa glanced over at her from time to time as they wrapped the presents, and she couldn't help thinking how wonderful she would have been as a mother. Some lucky child had lost out on her, all because she'd had her heart broken, irreparably it would seem, at a young age.

"Oh," Aunt Elaine uttered and rocked back on her heels. She'd been kneeling on the ground as she tried to smooth the wrapping paper over a box.

Melissa perked up right away and noticed the distorted look on her face. "Aunt Elaine? Are you okay?"

She waved her off. "I got a little woozy just now. Maybe all the kneeling and bending over."

"Are you sure you don't want to stop? I can do this on my own," Melissa offered. "Trust me. I have years of experience."

"Bah," Aunt Elaine muttered. "Probably just indigestion. I'll be fine."

"If you say so," Melissa replied, but she knew to keep a close eye on her. She wasn't as young and spritely as she once was, and even though she didn't know of her having any chronic illnesses or other health issues, it didn't mean she couldn't develop one.

They kept wrapping the gifts, but every now and again, Aunt Elaine would pause and tap her chest, her face all wrinkled up as if she'd just licked bitter lemon. Each time Melissa would ask, she'd pretend it was nothing.

Until she started sprouting beads of sweat.

"Okay, that's it," Melissa said and got up. "We're going to the doctor."

"Nonsense," Aunt Elaine protested. "I just need a little rest. I can lay down here for a couple of minutes."

"No can do," Melissa said and walked over to her, helping her to her feet. "I'll get your coat."

"Are you always this bossy?" Aunt Elaine grumbled as she shuffled after Melissa.

"Only when the people I care about don't listen to me," Melissa replied without looking.

Aunt Elaine followed her with a pout, and Melissa hurried upstairs to inform Gemma and Max they would be alone.

"Is she okay?" Gemma asked with worry in her eyes.

"I think so, but we just want to make sure," Melissa told the children. "I need for the two of you to be civil while we're gone. We shouldn't be long, but who knows? Just don't break anything else," Melissa pleaded with them.

"Okay," Max replied as he and Gemma shared a look of understanding.

"We'll be fine," Gemma promised. "Call me if you need anything."

"I will." Melissa smiled and returned downstairs. Aunt Elaine was sitting on the chair by the stairs, her face pale and her eyes looking more sunken than they had been moments before. "Let's go," she told her and helped her up.

Aunt Elaine was reluctant to go, and she sat stiffly in her seat in defiance. Melissa started to worry more as she drove down Main Street toward the doctor's office. It wasn't a busy day, which gave Melissa a lot of hope that they would see the doctor quickly before her aunt got any worse.

"I absolutely love this time of year," Melissa said as she saw the wreath on the entrance door and smelled the distinctive scent of green pinewood and cinnamon. Her stomach started to growl, and Aunt Elaine, perking up a little, started to laugh.

"Oh, that cheered you up, huh?"

"Yes," Aunt Elaine replied.

She wasn't looking much better, and Melissa hastened inside with her. The waiting room boasted a Christmas tree filled with red bows, candy canes, gold and silver strands of tinsel wrapped around the tree, and colorful lights that flickered, constantly making a kaleidoscope of colors on the wall.

Green garlands were draped along the oval reception area, and Melissa approached the bubbly receptionist wearing a red Christmas cap. "Hello?" she greeted them with a warm smile.

"Hi," Melissa responded, just as Aunt Elaine swooned in her arm.

"Oh," the woman gasped and ran around to the front of the desk. "What symptoms is she having?" the receptionist asked.

"She's flushing, and it seems she has stomach cramps. I'm not sure what's wrong," Melissa replied as she tried to keep Aunt Elaine tightly against her to prevent her from falling. "How soon can she see someone?"

"Come with me," the receptionist told her and hurried down the hallway to the nurse's station. "I have an emergency," she told the nurse and passed them off to the stocky nurse in the blue scrubs.

"Thanks, Marla," the nurse said and instantly led Aunt Elaine to the examination table. "Let me get her vitals," she said when Aunt Elaine was properly situated. "What's going on with her?" she asked Melissa, even though she wasn't looking at her.

"She's had some fainting spells, feeling woozy, and she's been complaining about her stomach, so I'm not sure if it's something she ate or what," Melissa replied.

"We'll see about that," the nurse said as she finished

her checks. "I'll let the doctor know what's going on. Please follow me."

She led them to a different examination room, where they were told to wait, and Melissa continued to monitor her aunt, who didn't seem to be doing much better.

About ten minutes later, the doctor came in. "Hi, I'm Dr. Weaver," he said with a toothy smile and extended his hand to Melissa.

"Hi," they responded simultaneously.

He sat on the stool and looked at Aunt Elaine. "I think your aunt may be a little dehydrated," he said. "We're going to get her a bed, some fluids, anti-nausea meds, and she'll be fine in no time, okay? But Miss Elaine, you're going to have to take your fluid intake seriously."

"Bah," she said and waved him off.

Melissa rolled her eyes. "This is what I have to put up with," she replied.

Dr. Weaver chuckled and stood. "Okay, ladies, follow me."

He led them to a small room in the facility, where the nurse returned to get Aunt Elaine set up with her medication. Once she was in bed and the saline drip was attached to her, they were left alone.

"I need to start monitoring your water intake, Auntie," Melissa scolded her. "I had no idea it was that bad."

"I think they're exaggerating," Aunt Elaine said as her denial set in.

"Yeah," Melissa replied sarcastically. "I'm sure that's what it is."

She sat next to her bed, already resigning on the day ahead. It would be a while before they'd be able to leave, so she settled into the chair and began to read one of her digital books to pass the time. She must have felt like

Aunt Elaine was watching her, but when she looked up after several pages, she was staring at her.

"What is it?" Melissa asked and laughed nervously.

"I was just wondering if I had a daughter if she'd have been like you," she mused.

"Maybe." Melissa shrugged. "It could happen if some things were the same. Like you and mom are sisters, so that's equal genes, so maybe if the guy was like dad..."

"He was," Aunt Elaine replied and sighed.

"He was like Dad?" Melissa asked and wrinkled her brows.

"Exactly like Dick," Elaine replied.

Melissa suddenly developed an unsettling feeling in the pit of her stomach. "I don't understand."

Aunt Elaine exhaled loudly. "Remember how I told you about that man I loved and lost? That was your father."

Melissa's jaw dropped, and her eyes bulged. "You're kidding."

"Nope," Aunt Elaine said. "I was in love with him, we made plans, and Betty came along and off they went. She got pregnant with you, and the rest is history."

Melissa couldn't believe what her aunt was telling her, but suddenly everything made sense. No wonder they couldn't get along. Her mother had stolen her aunt's boyfriend, and she was the thing between them.

"But how come you've been so nice to me all this time?" Melissa asked in shock.

"Because it had nothing to do with you, dear." Aunt Elaine smiled. "I sort of pretended you were my daughter too."

"I'm so sorry," Melissa said sadly. "I had no idea."

"Your mother tried to reach out to me over the years, but I wasn't up for it. I was still heartbroken."

"I can understand that," Melissa replied. "Finally."

"It wasn't something either of us was willing to talk about. She married the man I loved. The only man I'd loved. How do you start that conversation?"

"Yeah," Melissa said and sighed. "But you said Mom tried, right?"

"Yes, she did a couple of times," Aunt Elaine admitted.

"Now, who's self-sabotaging?" Melissa asked, throwing her words at her. "Why don't you reach out to her for a change? I'm sure she didn't mean to hurt you."

"There was a long time when I didn't think that at all," Aunt Elaine mumbled. "I was too hurt. But over the years, I could see that Dick really loved her, maybe more than he ever did me. They were happy, and I resented that sometimes too."

"That's normal, I think," Melissa told her. "So, how do you feel now?"

"I don't know. Maybe having you here with me gave me some clarity. I don't feel as terrible about it anymore."

"Good," Melissa said as a sneaky idea formed in her mind. She took out her phone and dialed her mother. "Mom?"

Aunt Elaine's eyes popped when she realized what she was doing, and she waved frantically in the background that she didn't want to talk.

"Too bad," Melissa mouthed back to her. "Mom, I have someone who wants to talk to you."

And instantly, all the color drained from Aunt Elaine's face.

Chapter Eighteen

"**W**ho is it?" Betty asked on the other end. "How's it going over there, by the way?"

"Everything's great, Mom," Melissa replied. "I can see you're having quite the celebration over there. Are you at a carnival?"

"Oh yes." Betty smiled. "Your father is somewhere over there," she said and pointed in the distance. "I don't know why he loves it so much, but he was the one who dragged me out here."

"Well, I'm glad you're both doing okay, but that's not why I called," Melissa replied as Aunt Elaine stared at her, her face aghast.

"Okay. What is it?" Betty asked. Melissa turned the phone to Aunt Elaine so they could see each other. "Oh," Betty replied less than enthusiastically.

Aunt Elaine was completely flushed. "Hi," she said, and Melissa snickered at the old woman who'd suddenly started to sound like a child.

"Are you in the hospital?" Betty asked in alarm,

almost as if the two sisters had been on speaking terms all along.

"Oh, nothing to worry about," Aunt Elaine replied. "Just dehydrated."

"Alright," Betty said. "Well, at least you're not alone."

"Yeah, she won't lay off of me." Aunt Elaine grinned and looked over at Melissa, who motioned to her to say something to Betty about why they hadn't been speaking.

"How are you really?" Betty asked, and Melissa could hear the relief in her mother's voice that Aunt Elaine was finally speaking to her.

"Let's not pretend this is normal, okay?" Aunt Elaine replied with a sigh. "I know that over the years, I haven't been...I wasn't willing to talk to you. And you know why."

"I know." Betty sighed too. "But I told you, I didn't mean to hurt you."

"I know you didn't, but for a long time, I was hurt, and I blamed you because I couldn't blame him. I never moved on."

"I can understand that," Betty added.

"Just let me finish before I change my mind," Aunt Elaine snapped. Melissa chuckled when she noticed the pinched look on her mother's face. "I was wrong. Yeah, you knew about me and Dick, but it wasn't you who made him fall in love with you, and I didn't get that for a long time. That's why I was always so close to Melissa because it was like my way of holding on to him. But I know it hurt you, too, when we drifted apart."

The room was quiet as both Melissa and Betty waited for their cue to speak. When Melissa glanced at the screen, her mother had tears rolling down her face.

"You have no idea how long I've waited for you to say that to me," she sniffled.

Aunt Elaine's eyes became glossy as well, and she tightened her lips as she fought the tears. Melissa felt the knot in her own stomach as her emotions overcame her.

"I know," Aunt Elaine finally managed to say. "But all this emotional bonding is going to dehydrate me some more."

Betty laughed. "Okay, fine. But can I call you back later to check on you?"

Aunt Elaine's eyes twinkled. "Sure thing."

"Alright, Mom," Melissa said and turned the phone so her mother could see her. "I'll call back later or when we get home. She should be out after this bag of whatever is in this solution."

Betty chuckled. "Okay, and thank you." She smiled. "I know Elaine can be stubborn, and so are you. I'm glad yours won this time."

"I can still hear you," Aunt Elaine called out, which led to the ladies erupting into laughter.

"Bye, Mom. Love you," Melissa told her mother before she hung up.

There was an awkward pause for a couple of seconds when Melissa just looked at her aunt, whose face seemed more content than she'd seen it in a while.

"Thank you." She smiled and said to her too. "This wouldn't have happened without you. I didn't know I could even do that."

"That's because she's your sister," Melissa said as she took her feeble hand. "You love her, even if you're mad at her. Besides, this happened a long time ago. It's way too long for a grudge if you ask me."

Aunt Elaine laughed. "You're probably right about that."

"Okay, let's get you rested so we can get out of here,"

Melissa said as she resumed her seat on the chair.

The room was quiet. Only the sounds of dripping and beeping interrupted the stillness as Melissa got lost in the crossword puzzles that she was eagerly trying to solve.

A few hours later, though Aunt Elaine was still feeling a little weak, she was discharged with strict orders to increase her liquid intake and get some rest. Melissa noticed how much stronger she was when they walked to the car.

"Maybe I should have asked Dr. Weaver for some of what he gave you for when my energy is low," she teased.

"Trust me. You don't want that willingly." She chuckled as Melissa opened the door for her to get in.

"I think I do," Melissa told her as she slid behind the wheel. "And when we get home, don't even think about helping me with the gifts or the tree. I'll ask the kids whether they want to or not. You are going to get some rest and a bath of water to drink."

Aunt Elaine snickered. "Aye, aye, captain."

She pulled into the driveway and helped her aunt to the door. As soon as it opened, the smell of sugar, cinnamon, and vanilla hit them, and they looked at each other in shock.

The house was enveloped with the sweet smell of baking, and Max hopped out from behind the partition, his shirt dusted with flour and his face displaying grains of sugar.

Melissa laughed. "What are you two doing?"

Gemma appeared behind Max, bearing a tray of gingerbread cookies. "A peace offering." She grinned. "I hear they work wonders."

Melissa's heart was full of gratitude to see they had finally come around. "Thank you," she said and hugged them as she took one and bit into it. "And they're good too."

"Well, I learned from the best." Gemma smirked.

"Hey, I thought that was me." Aunt Elaine chuckled as she took a cookie too. "Oh my," she said and licked her lips. "They taste a lot like mine."

Gemma did a little curtsy. "Thank you, ladies. I wasn't just here for my good looks. I picked up a thing or two."

"When?" Melissa asked with shock. "You never seem to want to be in the kitchen."

Gemma only smiled. "Don't you worry about that. There are many ways to learn," she said and returned to the kitchen before she rubbed her palms together and walked behind them to the living room. "How're you doing, Aunt Elaine?"

"I was just dehydrated," she told Gemma. "Nothing to worry about."

"Thank goodness for that," she replied.

But their surprise wasn't over. Melissa's jaw dropped to the floor when they saw the finished tree and all the gifts wrapped and placed under the tree.

She turned to Gemma and Max with tears in her eyes. "Really?"

Gemma and Max looked at each other before Max spoke. "We figured we'd been giving you a really hard time, so we thought we'd make up for it."

"Plus, Aunt Elaine isn't well, which means more pressure on you," Gemma added.

"Now, don't anyone feel sorry for me," Aunt Elaine chimed in. "I'll be fine."

"Ignore her," Melissa told them. "But thank you so much," she said and wiped a tear that had escaped. "This means the world to me." She walked over to her children and hugged them tightly. "I love you both so much."

"Love you too, Mom," they replied simultaneously.

Melissa's heart felt as if it had doubled over the past couple of minutes. She felt as if she was filled with helium and floating as she walked to the sofa. But even as she sat, she began to wonder if it wasn't all just a show. All it proved was that her kids could behave better, but she couldn't help but think that they were just trying to pacify her because she'd had a meltdown earlier and the fact that Aunt Elaine wasn't feeling well. She wasn't sure how long it would last, and the doubts crept in, pushing away all the pride she'd just felt.

She sank into the sofa, and from the corners of her eyes, she saw them stealing away upstairs. Aunt Elaine had started dozing off, and Melissa got up and shook her gently. "How about we get you to bed?"

Aunt Elaine didn't protest that time. She let Melissa lead her to her bedroom, where Melissa remained while she took a quick shower just in case she needed the help. After she had drunk some water and eaten a tuna salad, Aunt Elaine settled into bed.

Which left Melissa with nothing else to do. She was glad the kids had finished the work for her, but it also meant that there was nothing else for her to do. She was beat from the day she'd had, and she started to feel the fatigue sinking in.

She wasn't in the mood to cook, despite the house smelling so lovely. She settled for ordering pizza, which the children appreciated. They took their slices to their rooms, and Melissa sat on the sofa alone, barely tasting the food as she watched Christmas favorites on TV that she'd already seen a dozen times.

She dozed off, her eyes hardly able to stay open, and when she jumped up again, it was dark. The house was quiet, and the Christmas lights twinkled in the background. She got up and stretched before moving to the kitchen to dump the empty pizza box.

The stairs creaked as she walked upstairs, and she noticed that the lights weren't on in either Max's or Gemma's rooms. She narrowed her eyes as she looked from one door to the other. Surely, they hadn't already gone to sleep. It was only minutes past nine, and they were teenagers, after all, who didn't think sleep was necessary.

But anything was possible after the day she'd had. She got to her room and stripped down as she anticipated a soothing bath. It didn't turn out as she'd planned. Her mind was a jumbled maze of worry and concern so that by the time she got out of the bath, she felt tired.

"This is ridiculous," Melissa muttered to herself. She wished she could take the win, but she felt as if she was locked into a prison in her own mind.

She noticed, on the way back to her bedroom, that Max's light was on. That was more like it. But then, as she passed, she heard whispers coming from the room. The door was slightly ajar, and she could tell that Gemma was inside.

She hoped they weren't fixing to go another round of fighting. Melissa didn't have the energy to stop them. But what she heard wasn't fighting. They were whispering animatedly as if they were colluding on a plan. She wanted to listen in so she could discern what they were up to, but she decided against it. They weren't fighting, and that was more than she could have asked for.

She curled up in bed that night, and her mind drifted

to Ian. He had been a real source of support for her, even though he barely knew her. She hadn't spoken to him in two days, and she knew that the longer she waited to call him, the harder it would be for her to get the words out.

She fell asleep to thoughts of reconciling with him as her heart once again started to race, and she decided against calling him.

Chapter Nineteen

When morning broke on the horizon, Melissa knew she was going to have a slow day.

She wanted to get out of bed, but her body wanted to remain there. It was only a few days until Christmas, and she had a lot to do. She had to bake Christmas pudding, which meant she had to prep the fruits and nuts to add to it. Then there was the turkey, the minced pie, the cookies, the vegetables, and juices. Just thinking about it was giving her a headache.

But they all needed to get done. The menu was extensive, and she'd thought about it long before she'd gotten to Yuletide Creek, and she thought things would have been different— that she'd have help. The reality had proven otherwise, and with all she had to do, she was already feeling behind.

She dragged herself out of bed and was a little elated when she heard pots and pans clattering in the kitchen. Aunt Elaine was already up and shuffling around in the kitchen.

"Hey, what are you doing?"

"Did you see where I put the box of chamomile tea?" Aunt Elaine asked without looking at her.

"Hey, I'm talking to you," Melissa said more forcefully.

"Honey," Aunt Elaine said as she turned to her. "I was dehydrated. I didn't have brain surgery."

Melissa laughed. "I know, but shouldn't you be taking it easy anyway?"

"And just laying around doing nothing?" she asked and scrunched up her face. "Ah, here it is," she said as she recovered the box of tea. "Do you want some?"

Melissa sighed. She knew it was a losing battle going up against her aunt. "Sure. You're going to do whatever you want anyway."

Aunt Elaine smiled. "You must have gotten that stubborn streak from somewhere, right?"

"I guess." Melissa smirked and started turning around in the kitchen. She didn't know where to start or what to do first. Well, she knew what not to do— vegetables and salads. Those would have to wait for Christmas Day. What she could do was prep the roast, mince, and turkey. She could also start baking. "Hey, is anyone coming over for Christmas?" she stopped to ask.

"I don't know," Aunt Elaine replied and placed the cup of tea to her lips. She peered at Melissa with accusatory eyes over the rim of the cup. "Is there?"

Melissa groaned. "Okay, then no," she said.

Aunt Elaine shook her head in disbelief. "I can't believe we're related."

"What does that mean?" Melissa asked as the woman shuffled out of the kitchen.

"You wouldn't get it anyway," she told her.

But Melissa already knew what she meant. She still

hadn't spoken to Ian, and she knew her aunt was still disappointed in her for that. She sighed and headed for the pantry. There was no sense in thinking about that now. Ian was quickly becoming a distant memory. She knew she should have reached out to him after turning him away, but he hadn't made any efforts toward her either. Maybe he wasn't as invested in her, so what was the point?

She didn't want to stir things up by going to see him and apologizing. She was afraid he'd ask her out again, and she couldn't tell if she was ready for that. She had other things she needed to focus on. She couldn't be distracted by Ian, even if he was the nicest man in Yuletide Creek.

So, she set her mind to the work in front of her that she could actually do. To help in her mood and with her confused mind, she put on some Christmas music. Usually, that would cheer her up, and as she expected, soon, she was humming as she rubbed her marinade into the turkey and stuffed the pockets in the roast with herbs.

"Ooh, la la!" Gemma exclaimed when she walked into the kitchen. "Something smells awfully nice."

Melissa smiled. "Did you come just to admire my work or to help me out?"

"Uh," Gemma replied and scratched her head. "I just came to get water. And maybe juice. Where's breakfast?" she asked as she glanced over at the empty stove.

"You can make something for us," Melissa suggested.

Gemma groaned. "Why did I come down here?"

Melissa laughed. "Come on," she coaxed. "Remember how much fun we used to have in the kitchen making waffles from scratch?"

"Mom, that was like a decade ago," Gemma said and

rolled her eyes. She was wearing a hooded sweater and leggings, even though she was inside. "What I remember is eating all of those Christmas puddings."

"Ooh, there's something you can help me with after you make breakfast," Melissa said and didn't bother looking at her. She knew the kind of look she was receiving from Gemma, and she smiled to herself.

"*I'm* making breakfast? When did we agree on that? Besides, it's almost eleven. Who wants breakfast at eleven?"

"Me," Max said as he slid into the kitchen. He, too, was wearing a hooded pullover and jeans.

Melissa looked at them suspiciously. "Why are you two dressed like that?"

Max and Gemma looked down at themselves and then across at each other. "Like what?" Gemma asked.

"Like you're outside," Melissa said and gesticulated to them.

"Mom, it's cold," Gemma said and shook her head. "If I'm going outside, I'll need another jacket. And a hat. And scarf. And gloves."

"You know what I mean," Melissa told her. "Especially Max. He's always half dressed."

Max grinned. "House is cold."

Melissa shook her head and gave up. She knew better than to think she could win that one. "I still need help with something."

"Fine," Gemma moaned. "I'll help with the pudding."

"Thank you," Melissa said and rubbed her shoulder. "I'll get to it in a minute. You can make some sandwiches in the meantime."

"Nope," Gemma said. "Max is getting cereal, and so am I. Pudding is one too many tasks that I didn't plan for."

Melissa gasped mockingly. "You didn't plan on helping me with anything?"

"I mean, I'll help with the eating." Max smiled. "And maybe loading the dishwasher after."

"Wow," Gemma said and turned to him. "Typical boy."

"You're no better," Max said and poured some milk over his Froot Loops. "Mom had to beg you."

Gemma stuck her tongue out at him as he spooned some cereal into his mouth and took off. "World's greatest brother and son."

"Now you know how I feel all the time," Melissa quipped.

"Really, Mom?" Gemma asked and gave her mother a poker stare. "Low blow."

Melissa laughed. "Okay, I'm done with these," she said of the turkey and roast, now onto the mince. "I still need to get that seasoned. I'll let them sit until tomorrow, and then the cooking shall begin," she said dramatically.

"Why are we making so much food anyway? Who's coming over?"

"No one has to be coming over," Melissa told her and blushed. "But it's Christmas, and we need a variety of dishes."

"*Should* someone be coming over?" Gemma asked and raised her brows at her mother.

"Not you too," Melissa replied.

"I'm just saying," Gemma said and shrugged. "We don't need all this food if it's just us."

"At least I won't have to cook again until the New Year," Melissa told her, already feeling the guilt sink in.

She stood by the counter, pressed her palms against

the edge, and stared at Gemma. "Do you want me to invite him over?"

"I dunno," Gemma replied. "Up to you."

She wasn't helping. Aunt Elaine had been forceful about what she wanted Melissa to do, and Gemma had hinted at it too. Was she the only one with her head in the clouds?

She shook her head to dispel her mind of the thoughts that were plaguing her. She needed to distract herself from her mental torment. She was a klutz when it came to dating, and the last several attempts had proven that to her.

Gemma helped her prepare the pudding, but she disappeared soon after. Aunt Elaine was on the enclosed porch at the back in her rocking chair, and her throw draped across her lap. Melissa felt like the tormented spirit of the household. The tension from the past several days hung over the house like a shroud, and she shivered from its effects.

She'd been in Yuletide Creek and that house for long enough to know she couldn't hope for more. Her children weren't ignoring her as much, and there was something to say for that, but it was not the festive holiday she'd envisioned when she'd packed up and came to Yuletide Creek two weeks before.

There was nothing for her to do after she'd prepped the food, so she settled on sitting by the fire and cozying up to a good movie. That should cheer her up, at least.

She'd barely sat when Gemma bounded down the stairs, her eyes wild. "Mom, can I borrow your keys?"

"Keys?" Melissa asked and wrinkled her brows.

"Yeah. For the car," Gemma explained as if she was talking to a toddler.

"What for?" Melissa wanted to know. Gemma hadn't wanted the car since they'd been in Yuletide Creek. Her request was a little suspicious and caught Melissa off guard.

"I need to go into town," Gemma said.

"I can take you," Melissa said as she started to get up. She was more than happy to find something else to do than mope.

No! Gemma exclaimed. "Max and I are going gift shopping, so you can't be there."

"Oh," Melissa replied and sat back down. "Do you even know where to go?"

"I'll figure it out." She grinned.

"Okay. It's in my purse on the nightstand."

"Thanks," she said and hurried off. "We won't be long."

Melissa watched as she ran off, and she stood by the door and observed as Gemma backed out of the driveway and turned onto the street. She couldn't believe that her children had grown up that much. She didn't expect to be in Yuletide Creek for crowning moments like that. She sighed as she thought about how her life had veered dramatically off course.

It was nothing like she'd planned. So much had changed over the course of a few years that she was having difficulty finding herself in all the confusion and noise. But Yuletide Creek wasn't such a bad town. If she was going to start over, it wouldn't be the worst place to do it. Besides, it made a lot of sense for her to stick close to the only family that she had on that side of the hemisphere.

There was no telling if her parents would even return from Southeast Asia. Aunt Elaine and her children were all she had, and that thought alone drove deep-rooted loneliness in her that even she couldn't ignore or deny.

Her only concern would be the kids, but the more she thought about it, that was sort of working its way out. Gemma hadn't decided on what she wanted to do concerning college or a job. Max had been a socially awkward boy throughout middle and high school— he hadn't had many friends on account of his being so sensitive. Maybe he'd bond better when the environment was smaller.

As for her, she was pretty sure she could find a teaching job in town or close enough. That would give her a purpose once again. The more she thought about it, the more the idea took root inside her and became a decision.

Of course, being in Yuletide Creek came with its fair share of struggles. There was a certain man she had to make amends with. There was no way she could live there without running into him. Her aunt and daughter had been right— it was about time she stopped sabotaging herself. Her children didn't need her as much anymore, which meant it was time for her to think about herself.

Hermit or not, Ian deserved her apology. They didn't need to be an item for her to be human. She sighed and returned to the sofa as she began to think about the best way to apologize. After the time that had passed, he needed more than a basket of baked goods and a smile.

She'd make it right, and just the thought alone created such panic in her she almost choked on it. It also made her smile to think she could even have those feelings again.

But she loved it, and when she started watching the movie, he was all she could think about.

Chapter Twenty

Melissa had dozed off without knowing it, and she jumped up and looked around wildly. She was still alone and on the sofa.

She stretched and yawned as she got up and started walking out the kinks. Her eyes caught the clock, which read eighteen minutes after four.

She was heading to the kitchen when she noticed that the car wasn't in the driveway. "What on earth?" she said to herself as she wandered closer. Aunt Elaine had moved to the front porch and was eating a sandwich. "Auntie, have you heard from the kids?"

"No," she replied and looked up at Melissa. "What are you worried about? They'll be fine."

Melissa rubbed her shoulders and looked out at the light snow that was falling. "I guess," she said and joined Aunt Elaine on the chair swing. "It's just weird for them to be gone for so long. And together."

"That's strange?"

"Very." Melissa chuckled. "In case you haven't noticed, they are always at each other's throats."

Aunt Elaine laughed. "I haven't seen any red and blue lights lately, so I think they're safe so far. Maybe they grew up."

"That would be a nice thought." Melissa smiled. But she knew her children. They were up to something. Max and Gemma never hung out together, and especially not for over three hours in a small town. There weren't many department stores or gift shops in town, so gift shopping shouldn't have taken them that long.

The thought had barely left her mind when she spotted the car coming down the street.

"There they are, in one piece," Aunt Elaine mocked.

"I wished you had had your own children, and then you'd understand," Melissa told her.

Aunt Elaine laughed. "I guess I didn't miss that part of it. I got the good part with you."

"Lucky you," Melissa said as she watched her children get out of the car and hurry up the steps. What was noticeable was the lack of gift bags.

She narrowed her eyes at them as they walked onto the porch. "Gift shopping, huh?"

"Well, we're not going to bring them inside with you sitting right there. We haven't wrapped them yet," Gemma retorted.

"So suspicious," Max teased.

"By the way, we need the both of you to get dressed. We have a surprise for you," Gemma said animatedly.

Melissa turned to her aunt. "I told you they were up to something."

"Where are we going? Do I need to put on my dancing shoes?"

Max snickered and blushed. "Yeah, right."

"Nothing so dramatic. Just regular clothes," Gemma answered.

"Where are we going?" Melissa insisted and remained seated.

"Mom, why do you always want to ruin the fun? Just put on something warm, and let's go. I promise, it's a surprise you'll love."

Melissa sighed. She couldn't think of what surprise they could have planned in such a short space of time when they didn't know anywhere or anyone.

"Mom!" Max whined. "Come on."

"Okay, you can just take me if miss fuddy-duddy here doesn't want to go anywhere," Aunt Elaine said as she got up. "Be right back."

Melissa was anxious about what they had planned, and she didn't want to waste whatever efforts they'd expended on their little "surprise."

"Fine," she eventually said and got up. "But I better like it."

Their faces lit up at the same time as they ushered her inside. "Quick!" Gemma said excitedly. "You're going to be so happy you came."

Melissa's imagination ran rampant all the while she got dressed. She couldn't think of a single thing that made sense. As far as she knew, she'd missed many of the Christmas events happening in town, and she'd already gone to the ones she knew about.

What could Max and Gemma have planned for me?

She couldn't deny that their excitement had filtered into her consciousness, and when she returned downstairs, her heart was palpitating. "Fine, let's go before I change my mind."

"Alright," Gemma said and looped her arm through her mother's. Max did the same on the other side.

"You're scaring me."

Gemma laughed. "There's something else we need from the both of you," Gemma said as they got to the car.

"What now?" an irritated Melissa asked.

Both Gemma and Max fished out two bandannas and waved them at the ladies. "We need you both to wear these."

"Oh no," Melissa said and started backing off.

"What's the point of a surprise if you see it coming?" Gemma asked. "Mom, for once, just have a little fun."

Her words stung Melissa. She didn't want to come off as the boring parent. At least not anymore. She would just have to trust them.

"Okay," she said softly. "I'm trusting you not to dump me in a ditch somewhere."

Max laughed. "We wouldn't need all of this for that," he teased.

"What?" Melissa asked, much to the amusement of everyone else.

"Just get in," Gemma ordered her, and both she and Max blindfolded the ladies.

It was an uncomfortable ride for Melissa, and as much as she didn't know the town like the back of her hand, it didn't stop her from trying to count the turns as she tried to determine where Gemma and Max were taking her.

"Are we there yet?" Melissa asked when it seemed as if the ride was taking too long.

Gemma snickered. "If we were there, I wouldn't still be driving."

Gemma had never taken her anywhere before, and that alone was a reason for Melissa to be proud, but she couldn't get a handle on that. She was too panic-stricken to care about anything but the impending surprise, which she hoped she would like and not cause further panic.

"I hope this didn't cost too much," Melissa said by way of trying to determine if they'd used her credit cards to do something she wouldn't approve of. That would ruin the surprise for her.

"Mom, just relax," Gemma said. "It's all good."

Aunt Elaine chuckled. "This is the most fun I've had in a while."

"See? Even Aunt Elaine is enjoying this part," Gemma added. "Okay, we're here," Gemma said, and the car came to a stop. "Don't take off the blindfolds," she commanded as she and Max hopped out of the car.

Gemma took her mother's hand, and Max led Aunt Elaine for a short way before they stopped. Melissa shivered when she heard them heave.

"Now?" she asked.

"Now," they replied simultaneously and started giggling.

Melissa couldn't get the blindfold off fast enough, and she gasped when she did and then covered her mouth. "Oh my god!"

"So?" Max asked excitedly as he sported a wide grin.

They were in Ian's tree lot, and all the trees were decorated to the nines. There were white lights covering every tree, and blue, red, and green ornaments, bells, whistles, and bows hung from the branches. The light snow falling in the background made her feel as if she'd just stepped into a snow globe. And to top it off, Ian was standing by the entrance wearing a Santa suit, which only made her laugh through the happy tears that had welled up in her eyes.

"Did you do this?" she asked the kids.

"Yep," Max replied.

"Wow!" Aunt Elaine exclaimed. "I've never seen this place looking like this."

"You said you wanted a memorable Christmas, and I don't think it can get more memorable than this," Gemma boasted and threw her arm around her mother's neck.

"You got that right," Melissa told her. "And there I was forcing you two to help with the one tree at home, and you came here and decorated an entire lot in a couple of hours?"

"Mom, don't ruin it," Gemma replied.

"Okay, fine. You're right. I really appreciate this," Melissa apologized. "This is absolutely amazing."

"Come on," Aunt Elaine said to the kids. "Let's go check out all these lights."

Melissa knew exactly what she was doing— giving her space to talk to Ian. If she thought she wasn't ready, it was too late to do anything about it. She sucked in a deep breath as she walked off to meet him.

"So, how'd you like the surprise?" he asked, without a mention of her horrible attitude and rudeness.

"Ian, I'm so sorry for how I acted the last time I saw you. I was going through a lot with the kids, and I didn't think I could handle..."

"Hey!" he said and stopped her. "It's fine. I get it. You've been through a lot, and I, for one, know exactly how that feels. It's not like we were engaged or anything."

"Why are you so nice to me?" she asked without thinking.

"Maybe because we all deserve a little bit of that. Besides, I'm a nice guy. Can't you tell?" he asked as he smiled, and the wrinkles formed in his eyes. It tugged at her heart, and instantly she had the urge to kiss him, and it took every ounce of her strength to remain a lady.

"I can see that," she said, and she felt her cheeks warming from the blush.

"Plus, your kids told me they were to be blamed for you kicking me out the door," he said playfully as he stuffed his hands inside his pockets and rocked on his heels.

"Still, I don't know how they twisted your arm into something like this," she said and indicated the trees.

"They made a pretty good case. Something about their rotten behavior and how their mother needed cheering up and..."

"Oh my god." Melissa giggled and blushed. "They didn't."

"They did." He laughed. "I thought it was really sweet, and the trees were just here. You don't want to know how many people have come in to see them since. I think I can make it a yearly thing."

"That would be a good idea," she agreed.

"Maybe you can get to see them every year," he said.

She knew what he was insinuating, but she was already leaning in that direction, so it wasn't hard for her mind to run away with that thought. "Maybe," she said in a flirtatious way. Maybe I can get a personal tour next time."

"You can get one right now." He grinned.

"Okay," she said as they walked side by side into the lot. "I can't believe how nice you're being to me when I've been nothing but awful to you."

He laughed out loud. "If that's what you call awful, I'll take it. Makes me think you're a saint on a normal basis."

"Far from it," Melissa replied and swept her hair behind her ear playfully. "But I take the compliment."

They walked upon Max as he was checking out his handiwork, and she got panicky that he might be offended by her and Ian again. Instead, he just smiled and moved on. She should have known. They'd basically given her the go-ahead to date again.

"So, I guess with the tree lot closing soon, you're going back into hiding up in the hills."

He snickered. "Yeah, but if this beautiful woman I met a while back wants to, she can persuade me to come down for lunch in the park anytime."

"Hey, I can't make any promises, but that would be nice," she told him. "I mean, I do make a mean roast beef sandwich."

He chuckled boisterously. "I bet."

She couldn't make any commitments to him, but it felt as if there was something happening between them. From the little she knew about him, he'd be perfect for her. But she didn't want to get ahead of herself.

They walked side by side through the maze of lights and the gently falling snow falling. It was one of the most beautiful evenings she had ever had, under the stars, snow, and Christmas lights. It wasn't an evening she'd forget soon, and deep down, she hoped there would be many more of those moments between them.

In fact, the feelings didn't feel so deep down at all.

Chapter Twenty-One

Melissa woke up the following morning with a big smile.

She didn't know why she'd waited so long to say anything to Ian. Nothing was concrete between them, but at least the potential was there. And it made her happy.

"Oh, you're in a good mood this morning." Gemma smiled as she burst into the bedroom bearing her laptop.

"What's this?"

Gemma plopped down onto the bed without an invitation. "So, remember how I told you that I wasn't sure about college?"

"Yes, and I still don't feel so great about that idea," Melissa interrupted.

"Yeah, yeah, I know," Gemma said and waved her off as she continued to scroll down the screen, her eyes fixed on the page. "But I still need to find that thing that I can do, right?"

"Agreed," Melissa said and pulled her legs under her as she sat upright. "What were you thinking?"

"I don't know," Gemma said and glanced across at her mother.

"By the way, before we get into all of this, I didn't tell you how much I appreciated what you and Max did yesterday. You not only mended what I'd almost broken with Ian, but that was very thoughtful of you."

Gemma groaned. "You're welcome. Everyone was getting annoyed with you moping around the house as if your dog died."

Melissa's eyes popped, and then she started laughing. "Seriously?"

"Yes, seriously. Plus, we've kinda been hard on you since we got here, and we figured it wasn't nice."

"Wait, the other night, I passed Max's room and heard you two conspiring. Was that what you were planning?"

"You heard us?" Gemma asked in shock.

"No, I didn't hear what you were talking about," Melissa replied quickly before she got the idea in her head that she was listening in on their conversation. "I just noticed the two of you together and thought it was weird. You know how I feel about privacy."

"Anyway, yeah, that's what we were talking about. But back to what I came in here about," Gemma said as she began to get flustered.

"Okay, focus." Melissa smiled. So many times over the years, she'd felt as if she'd been doing a bad job with her children but looking at the young woman sitting in front of her, she couldn't be prouder. She hadn't done so badly, after all, especially considering all she'd had to endure after the divorce and with no idea how she'd navigate single parenthood.

"So, I wasn't sure what I was looking for," Gemma

began again, "but then I stumbled across some organizations that were doing humanitarian work around the world, like The Red Cross, or Salvation Army, and some other animal rights and nature preserves group, and I started to get interested in that kind of thing."

"Wait, humanitarian work worldwide? Does that mean you plan on shipping out?" Melissa asked in dismay.

"Yeah," she said softly. "I want to get involved in causes— find some real purpose for my life that actually helps other people or the planet, rather than being just one more accountant or business owner."

"I understand that, and what you're saying would make any mother proud. And I am. But I'm stuck on a worldwide cause, meaning leaving me."

Gemma turned to her mother and started giggling. "You should see your face."

"Of course," Melissa exclaimed. "My baby girl is thinking of going off on her own to some strange place."

Gemma looked at her and started laughing. "Mom, don't be so dramatic. When we came to Yuletide Creek, we didn't know anything about the Pacific Northwest in our own country, and so far, we seem to be doing okay. That's what gave me the idea that I could do the same thing anywhere in the world."

"Are you kidding me? I gave you the tool to leave me?" Melissa asked with dismay.

Gemma snickered. "I'm not dying, and it's not space exploration. We can video call."

"Still," Melissa said softly. "So, what were you thinking?" She wasn't ready for Gemma to be globetrotting, but if she was going to do it, then she might as well be involved in the process.

"How about this one?" Gemma asked. She turned the computer toward her mother so she could see what she was looking at. Melissa squinted as she tried to read the words on the screen. "I checked out a couple of causes, but this one is based in Southeast Asia."

"What? That's on the other side of the world!" Melissa said and looked across at Gemma with maternal concern.

"But it's where Grandma and Grandpa are, so if anything happens, they'll be close by," Gemma explained.

Melissa sighed. "I know you don't need my permission, but isn't there something in the US?"

Gemma laughed. "What's the difference? If I went to California, you wouldn't see me anymore. It would be the same thing."

"But you'd be closer. I could hop on a plane and come see you," Melissa said. "I don't even have a visa to go to any Asian country."

"Then get one," Melissa replied. "You could come and see us on the holidays."

Melissa sighed. "Okay, fine. I'll consider it, but I'm not loving this grand idea of saving the other side of the world. This half needs saving too."

Gemma giggled. "I'll probably get back to this side later, but I'm excited about this. It's something I really want to do."

"I can see that." Melissa smiled and stroked her face. Gemma was in a good mood, and as they sat there, she got the idea that it would be a good time to probe for information about Max. "So, you and Max talk, right?"

Gemma narrowed her eyes at her. "What do you mean if we talk? Of course, we talk."

"Not like that," Melissa corrected her. "I mean about feelings."

"Feelings? You think Max and I would really sit down and talk about our feelings?" She chuckled. "Mom, that's not even normal."

"What I mean is," Melissa said and slid to the edge of the bed next to Gemma. "I know that something is going on with him. He wasn't always this closed off."

"Are we talking about the same boy? Yea high, dirty blond hair, annoying?" Gemma asked as she held her hand up to demonstrate the height.

Melissa snickered. "Yes."

"Max has always been like that," Gemma said, as if it was public knowledge.

"Well, hasn't he seemed a little more distant lately, though," Melissa probed.

"Uh, not really." Gemma shrugged. "I mean, he doesn't really know anyone here. What else is he supposed to do?"

Melissa sighed. "Tell me if I'm wrong, but I thought something was eating at him when he was keeping your secret. I figured that was why he was grumpy all the time, but then that secret was out, and nothing had changed. I know something is wrong with him, and I won't get it out of him, so I assumed you would know something that would help me to understand what's going on with him."

Gemma exhaled loudly and closed her computer screen. "Mom, this may come as a surprise to you, but Max is good with having no friends. He doesn't mind staying by himself. All the while, back home, he was bullied by the other kids in school because he wasn't like them. He loved animals and seemed too sensitive, so they mocked him and called him names."

Melissa's jaw dropped. "He was bullied? Why didn't I hear about any of this before?"

"Because you're a parent who might go down to the school and just make things a whole lot worse for him," Gemma explained. "And then Dad left, and Dad was the one who he was sort of closer to, so that didn't help either."

Melissa's heart sank. She knew her children had felt the weight of the loss of their father, but she hadn't realized just how much it had impacted them, which only made her angry. Peter had completely abandoned his children and had left a gaping hole inside them that he didn't seem keen on mending. He hadn't reached out to ask about them. It was as if they were dead to him. She wouldn't stand for it especially considering the information Gemma had just shared with her.

"No wonder he didn't talk about any friends of his," Melissa groaned as realization hit her. "How could I have missed that?"

"Mom, don't beat yourself up over that. You had a lot going on, and so did we. I guess we just all had to find a way to figure things out on our own," Gemma replied, sounding more like a grown-up every day.

"That's no excuse. His father left, and I wasn't the best mother," Melissa replied sadly.

Gemma sighed. "See why we don't share some things? You get overly dramatic about it. Max is fine. Really."

Melissa wasn't convinced. "He doesn't look so fine, but at least now I get it."

"Max just doesn't know anyone, and I can tell you, he isn't so bummed out about being here," Gemma said and shook her head for emphasis. "At least now he gets a fresh start. He can make new friends. By the way, are you staying here? I wasn't sure even though you'd practically packed up the entire house before we left."

"I'm thinking about it," Melissa replied. "I'm more convinced now than before. At least a change in the environment did him some good. A new school might be a pretty good idea to him right now."

"I'm sure it will. Plus, this is a small town. Weird is the norm." Gemma giggled. "He won't look like such a goofball for having an ant farm or chasing frogs down by the stream."

Melissa chuckled as she began to feel much better. "I guess not." Her mind drifted to past Christmases when everything seemed great. "Do you remember that time we went to Canada for the holidays and took the ski lift to the top of the slope?"

Gemma immediately started laughing. "You mean that time when you gripped the rail so hard your hand almost froze?"

Melissa laughed too. "That very one. It looked like such an adventurous thing to do on the ground, but when I was in the air and looked down and saw all of that snow so far below, all I could see was me falling to my death."

"Well, it was snow, so maybe you wouldn't have died. Probably been a paraplegic," Gemma teased.

"What?" Melissa said and erupted into laughter again. "How is that not worse?"

"That was my point." Gemma grinned. "There are worse things in the world than dying, such as us sitting here talking about a life we once had."

"You're so right about that. How about we make some new memories?" Melissa asked her with a smile.

"Way ahead of you," Gemma said and indicated her

laptop. "I'm going to see about this organization. Maybe I can still get into their program."

"I meant together," Melissa moaned. "Not you off making memories by yourself."

"I'll send pictures, and then we can all share." Gemma beamed. "Plus, there was that tree lot thing last night."

"Yeah." Melissa smiled and blushed as she remembered being with Ian.

"He actually is a great guy, you know," Gemma said.

"I know," Melissa replied. "But *we* aren't talking about that right now. How about we go find Max and see what holiday plans he has? Maybe we can get him to wear a Christmas outfit too."

Gemma groaned and got up. "I forgot about that. Is it too late to back out of that deal?"

"Nope. You already got your side of the bargain. And just to think," Melissa said as she threw her arm around Gemma's shoulder and they walked out of the bedroom, "you could have escaped it if you'd been honest, to begin with."

"Don't remind me."

"Max!" Melissa called when she saw him returning to his room with what looked like a bowl of cereal. He stopped and stared at them with deer eyes. "How about some holiday activities for the family?"

He stared at them as if they had horns. "No thanks," he said and walked to his room, where he proceeded to close the door.

"Good luck with that," Gemma said and patted her mother's shoulder as she, too, disappeared into her room.

And Melissa was left wondering what she'd done wrong.

Chapter Twenty-Two

What Gemma told Melissa rocked her to the core.

She knew Max had been close to his father, but she'd never guessed he'd been going through so much, especially at school. She began to feel even more frustrated that Peter had abandoned his role as a father, and with a heaving chest and trembling fingers, she decided to give him a call.

She'd promised herself before that she would never call him— not after the way he'd walked out on them without as much as a cursory glance backward. But not after the devastation she had to witness daily when she looked at their son.

The phone started to ring, and her heart felt as if it was going to leap from her chest. It rang until the voice-mail kicked in without an answer. And she dialed it again.

"Hello?" his voice came over on the other end, and Melissa's heart did a flip-flop. It had been so long since she'd heard his voice that it paralyzed her.

"Uh, hello," Melissa replied.

There was a pause before he spoke again. "Melissa?"

She rolled her eyes. They'd lived together for over twenty years, and he was acting as if he didn't know what she sounded like. "Yes!" she said emphatically before she closed her eyes and reminded herself that the call wasn't about her. It was about Max and Gemma.

"Oh," his deep baritone responded. And then there was silence.

No questions. No comments. Just the sound of him breathing on the other end.

She wanted to throttle him. "You remember Max and Gemma, right? Your children?"

"Melissa, I don't want to start something with you right now. I was just heading out, and I have some appointments to keep."

"Start something? That's a good idea," she fired back, totally forgetting her plan to remain composed. She walked over to her bedroom door and closed it so the kids wouldn't happen to hear her arguing with him, of all people. "How about you start acting like these children belong to you too? I didn't call to argue with you, Peter. I called to ask you to care about them."

"And you think I don't care?" he fired back.

Melissa almost choked. "You have a funny way to show it. You walked out on me and forgot all about them. Not a single call from you. It's Christmas! Did you even plan on calling them ever again?"

"Melissa, I just can't handle the stress and the arguing," he replied in a weak attempt at pity.

"This is what disappoints me the most about you. I don't care if you never want to talk to me. Gemma and Max have their own phones. You can call them. Do you even know what Max has gone through since you left?"

Her chest was burning, along with her eyes as the tears threatened to fall.

"How is he?" he asked with a sigh.

"How about you call him and talk to him?" Melissa offered. She hated that she had to be forcing their father to want to have a relationship with them.

"Fine," he said. "I should have done that a long time ago. Send me his number. I'll call him now."

"Thank you," Melissa replied, feeling a little relieved that he'd finally agreed.

She hung up the phone and immediately walked across the hall to Max's room. "Hey," she said to him.

He looked up from his phone. "Hey."

"So, I have some great news," she said and sat next to him. "I just spoke to your dad, and he said he'll be calling you in another couple of minutes."

Max's face instantly lit up. "Really?" he asked and sat upright, his phone immediately forgotten. "When did you talk to him? What did he say? Is he going to come here?"

The questions flooded from him like a leaky pipe, and Melissa was a little jealous at how such a simple statement about his dad had evoked more promise and joy than all her efforts combined. "Slow down, tiger," she said and smiled weakly as she grappled with the overwhelming emotions of the moment. "I just talked to him, so listen out for his call."

Max picked up the phone again, and though Melissa was grateful that he was finally smiling, she couldn't help but feel anxious and apprehensive. She was dealing with Peter, after all, and he was a wild card.

Melissa's heart was nonetheless lifted as she walked to the kitchen to get started on the foods she'd already prepared. Aunt Elaine had already started with the pudding, and the house was filled with the sweet aroma of cinnamon and spices.

"Oh my goodness, I could eat that right now," Melissa gushed as her stomach started rumbling.

"Me too," the old woman replied. "We just have to wait like everybody else."

"So, I have some good news," Melissa said as she removed the foil pan from the fridge.

"Oh?" Aunt Elaine replied in a suggestive voice as she shuffled closer to Melissa.

"It's not about Ian." Melissa laughed.

"Psshh!" Aunt Elaine hissed and waved her off. "What then?"

"I finally spoke to Peter, and he agreed to call Max and wish him Merry Christmas or talk to him anyway."

"Oh, wow! That's a nice surprise. He must be excited." Aunt Elaine smiled.

"More than I realized he would be," Melissa admitted. "I knew he must've missed him, but the way his face lit up— that was a total shock for me. I thought he would have been as indifferent to him as he is to me."

Aunt Elaine laughed. "I bet that bruised your ego a bit."

"Tell me about it," Melissa said and walked over to the oven to preheat it. "At least he's excited about it. Maybe after this, he will be more sociable. I just wish he could be more involved in their lives."

"You don't get to choose that, unfortunately," Aunt Elaine told her. "At this point, you take what you can get."

"I guess," Melissa agreed.

The women busied themselves in the kitchen for the remainder of the day. Melissa assumed Max and Peter had already spoken, but she was surprised when evening rolled around, and Max didn't come bounding down the stairs with joy.

Melissa's back was starting to ache from all the bending and stretching, but they were done with everything. The salads would be taken care of on Christmas, and with the day looming over them, Melissa began to feel the excitement of the moment.

"I can't believe it's Christmas tomorrow," she said as she started dancing around the kitchen, her aching back forgotten.

"Thanks to all of you, I won't be spending it alone this year," Aunt Elaine commented as she sipped from her glass of apple cider.

"Aww," Melissa crooned. "Glad we could be of service." Max scurried down the stairs just then with a forlorn look on his face. "What is it?" Melissa asked as he dampened her festive mood.

"I thought you said Dad was going to call me," he said and held up his phone.

"He hasn't?" Melissa asked with shock and immediately dialed Peter's number. It rang several times without an answer. "I'm not getting him. I'm sorry, Max," Melissa said as she walked over to the distraught boy. "Maybe he'll call tomorrow instead."

"He won't!" Max blurted out. "He hasn't called one time! Not once!"

"Maybe he will this time," Aunt Elaine said softly.

"He won't!" Max insisted as the tears started rolling down his face. "He hasn't called at all. Why? What did I do?"

"Honey, you didn't do anything," Melissa said as she approached him.

Max wasn't having it. He backed away, and before

Melissa could say another word, he ran through the front door.

"Max!" she yelled after him as she bolted to the front door. She opened it just in time to see him sprinting across the yard and into the dark forest. "Max!"

"What's going on?" Gemma flew down the stairs and asked with panic in her eyes and voice.

"Max ran off," Melissa said as she grabbed her jacket and rushed outside. "Max!" she yelled again, her fear setting in as easily as the cold.

"Mom!" Gemma called after her. "Where are you going?"

"After him," Melissa replied. "It's dark, and he doesn't even know where he's going."

"Neither do you," Gemma reminded her.

"But I can't just leave him alone out there," Melissa said as her heart thudded so loudly that she could barely hear her own thoughts.

"Okay, I'll come with you," Gemma told her. "It doesn't make any sense if the two of you get lost. But why's Max mad?"

"His father promised to call and didn't," Melissa told her.

"When did you talk to him?" Gemma asked as she threw her coat around her shoulder.

"This morning. He asked for his number, and I gave it to him, and he said he'd call."

Gemma sighed. "Typical, as if he wasn't hurt enough as it was."

"Exactly," Melissa said and tried to see further into the darkness of the forest.

"Maybe you should call the cops," Aunt Elaine suggested.

"No!" Melissa shouted back. "I don't think it's that bad. Plus, it's Christmas Eve. I'm sure he's around here somewhere."

The two stayed close as they walked through the dark blanket of night. Luckily, there were no leaves on the trees — just the skeletons, which would make it easier to spot Max.

"Max!" Melissa cupped her hands at her mouth and shouted. "Max!"

Gemma did the same. They were so loud they were convinced all of Yuletide Creek must have heard them. But still, no trace of Max.

"I wonder if he left the woods and went out onto the street," Melissa wondered as she hugged herself against the icy chill. The snow was still fresh on the ground, and their feet crunched under them as they walked, calling for Max.

"He couldn't have gotten this far," Gemma finally said after what felt like an hour of searching.

"He must be here!" Melissa said in a state of panic. "What if something happens to him?"

"Mom!" Gemma said and gripped her by the shoulders. "Nothing's going to happen to him. He probably just needs a minute to cool his head. I'm sure he'll come back home when he's ready."

"What if he doesn't?" Melissa asked and brushed away fresh tears. "He was already hurting. What if this pushes him over the edge?"

"Mom, stop thinking about the worst case," Gemma said with annoyance. "I want to find him, too, but this is counterproductive. Just take a deep breath."

Melissa did as she was told, but she didn't feel any

better. She looked around her, but all she could see was darkness. "He must be so scared."

"Tell you what," Gemma said to her. "How about we call someone? Ian maybe," she said. "He probably knows these woods and can actually track Max instead of walking around in circles."

Melissa shook her head in agreement. "We can do that."

"Good." Gemma sighed with relief. "We agree on something. Call him."

Melissa was shaking when she took out the phone and dialed Ian's number. She wasn't sure if it was fear or the cold, or a combination of both, but she was going out of her mind by the time Ian answered the phone.

"This is a nice surprise," he said as he answered the phone.

"Max ran away!"

Chapter Twenty-Three

"What do you mean he ran away? Where are you?" Ian asked with urgency.

"He was home, and he got upset and ran outside and into the woods, and now we can't find him," Melissa rambled as she turned about in confusion. She was getting more frightened by the minute. She couldn't remember if she'd seen him wearing a jacket. He could be freezing.

"Okay, don't panic, okay? Chances are he's not too far. I'll be there in a few," he said and hung up.

Melissa couldn't help the tears that flooded her cheeks. She'd tried so hard to be there for her children, but one promised call from Peter had ripped the carpet from under her and had sent her sprawling on the floor once again. At Max's expense.

"This isn't happening," she said as she paced.

"Maybe we should go back to the yard to wait on Ian," Gemma suggested. "Who knows? Maybe Max went back home another way."

"That's a comforting thought," Melissa said as they backtracked the way home.

There was no sign of Max when they made it back to the yard, but a couple of minutes later, Ian's truck pulled up along the curb. He hopped out and rushed to her side. "Where did he go?"

"That way," Melissa said through clenched teeth.

Ian immediately took off in the direction Melissa showed him with both Melissa and Gemma in tow. He paused when he got to the edge of the woods and started walking slowly. "Did you both come through here before?" he asked as he shone his flashlight on the path.

"Yeah, we did," Melissa replied.

He slowed his pace and started searching for Max's tracks. "He went this way," he said and hurried through the thicket of trees. "How long has he been out here?"

"Not long before I called you," Melissa said breathlessly as she tried to keep pace. Gemma was right behind Ian as she tried to look for the tracks that he kept spotting.

"I don't know how you see anything," Gemma said.

"It's easier to track in the snow, as long as it isn't still falling," Ian explained. "Over here," he said and hurried down a path.

Melissa's heart leaped when they saw Max curled up next to a tree with his legs pulled up under him and his chin resting on his knees. "Max!" she exclaimed and descended upon him. "Why did you scare me like that?" she asked and hugged him.

"Hey, son," Ian said as he knelt next to Max. "Are you okay, buddy?"

Max simply nodded. "I didn't mean to scare anybody or run away. I just didn't want to talk to anyone."

"Oh, honey, I understand that," Melissa said. "But this was scary."

"Sorry," he muttered.

"Do you want to talk?" Ian asked him, taking on the father role to mend the hole caused by his actual father.

"It's just that I really miss him. I do, and he just doesn't seem to miss me. He said he'd call, and he didn't. Why doesn't he love me? I wish I could hate him too," he said and wiped away fresh tears as he looked away.

"I don't think he hates you," Ian replied softly and sat next to him. "I know it hurts because you miss him, but sometimes, the people we love choose a life without us, and there's nothing we can do about that. But you know what you can do?" he asked, and Max slowly turned his head to face him.

"What?"

"We can try to have our best life without them." He smiled. "It sucks that he's not around, but you know who is? These women who are out here in the cold hunting you down to make sure you're okay. They are the ones you focus on. Not the hurt. That might help."

Melissa's heart melted as she listened to Ian talking to Max with all the fatherly love he could muster. She'd never heard him mention children, but if he didn't have any, that was too bad— he'd have made a great father.

"So, do you think we can get out of this cold now?" Ian grinned and stood as he held out his hand for Max. He took it and rose right before Melissa ruffled his hair, and Gemma hugged him.

"You're going to be alright, little bro." She smiled. "But the next time you do that, I'm not leaving my nice warm bed to come out here to find you."

Max smirked. "Deal."

They all walked back to the house, where Aunt Elaine was beside herself with worry. "I'm so glad," she said as she greeted them by the door. "Why'd you go and do a thing like that?" she asked Max.

He shrugged and blushed. "I wasn't thinking."

"You're sure right about that," Aunt Elaine scolded. "You made us sick with worry."

"Auntie," Melissa called to her softly and gestured for her to stop. She knew Max already felt bad about what he'd done. She didn't want him feeling worse, so he'd go and lock up in his bedroom and mope again.

"I guess some hot cocoa would do everyone some good right now, huh?" Aunt Elaine asked and headed into the kitchen. "Come on in."

"Ian," Melissa said and pulled him aside. "Would you mind hanging around for a bit? I want to talk to the kids a little."

"Sure," he said and started looking around uncomfortably. "Where do I...?"

"Oh, you can wait in the living room," she said and led him there.

Max, Gemma, and Aunt Elaine were in the large kitchen. Gemma and Max were seated by the table as Aunt Elaine took out the teacups. In a couple of minutes, the kettle whistled, and she poured the hot cocoa into each cup.

Max still had a dazed look as he sipped his, and Gemma seemed to have contracted it too. Melissa sighed as she sat beside them.

"I know things have been hard," she began and started fidgeting with the cup. "When Peter left, it broke me." It was the first time she'd said those words aloud to her children. "I had so many things planned for my life. For your lives. And then, one day, I got up, and I was alone, and I thought the feeling would pass. But it didn't. And every day, I had to kick myself to get going. I was devastated and heartbroken. And I had to be a parent alone. I tried so hard to make life easier for the both of you, but I guess I didn't do such a good job of that."

"Nonsense," Aunt Elaine chimed in. "You did great with what you were left with," she insisted.

"Mom, you weren't the only one hurting." Gemma sighed. "I know I acted tough like it didn't bother me, but I hated him for leaving. That's why I was always so indifferent to him and his phone calls. I saw the way it ate at you— how you stopped smiling for so long. I heard you crying in the shower."

Tears rolled down Melissa's face. "You did? I didn't want you to see that."

Gemma started crying too. "Mom, you're human. I was locked in my room crying. Max was doing the same."

"I tried calling him a couple of times and didn't get him," Max added. "I missed him, and I wanted him to come home. But he never answered his phone. I didn't want you to know how much I missed him because I didn't want you to feel bad about it."

Melissa gasped. "Max, he's your father. You don't need my permission to miss him!"

"I know, but you would feel bad about it. You hated him," Max said sadly.

"I didn't hate him," Melissa corrected him. "I hated what he did to us."

"Yeah," Gemma agreed. "I don't want to talk to him, though. If he wants to stay away, then so be it. I'm just angry that he keeps messing with Max's head," Gemma said protectively.

Melissa had never seen her so defensive of Max. Maybe their little trip in the woods had done them some good after all.

"Well, I say good riddance to bad rubbish," Aunt Elaine quipped. "He was no good, and I'm sorry for saying that, but that's just the way I feel."

"No need to feel sorry," Melissa told her. "I think we all share the same sentiments."

"Yep," Gemma said and sipped her cocoa.

The family had never sat down and talked about how they felt after Peter left. They'd all just gone about their lives as if nothing had changed when in fact, everything had.

"I'm just so glad that we have each other," Melissa said to them. "Or I'm not sure what I would have done all this time."

"It may not look much like it, but we appreciate all the effort you've made," Gemma said, with a smile.

"Yeah," Max said and stared into the cup. "We give you a lot of crap."

Melissa laughed through new tears. "I know that much, and I always thought it was because you were hurting, so I understood."

"Didn't make it any easier, though," Gemma said. "Tonight was a big example. We don't consider you enough."

"This is heavy stuff," Melissa said as she sucked in a deep breath. "Let's just promise to be more considerate of the others in this family. We should talk more, for one, because if we had done this a long time ago, we could have started the healing process."

"We can start here," Gemma replied. "Okay, bring it in."

The trio moved closer as they hugged each other under the watchful and proud eyes of Aunt Elaine. The conversation had struck an emotional chord inside her as well, and Melissa noticed when she turned away and wiped the corners of her eyes.

Her heart was overflowing with joy as she hugged her children. She felt as if she'd gotten them back. "Listen, we've come a long way," Melissa said as they still held each other over the table. "We are stronger together because of it."

"Yeah," they replied simultaneously.

"Alright, how about we do something lighter," Melissa said in a shaky voice. This has been too emotional even for me."

Gemma laughed. "That works for me. What were you thinking?"

The trio pulled back. "Well, it's Christmas Eve. How about we watch a Christmas movie?" Melissa asked.

Ordinarily, Max and Gemma would have preferred to hide away in their rooms, but they glanced across at each other and smiled.

"Yeah, that works," Max replied. "But I'm choosing the movie," he said and ran off.

"I'm not watching *Elf!*" Gemma shouted after him, and the two started off in a race for the remote.

"Hey, watch it!" Melissa called after them.

"Let them be," Aunt Elaine told her. "That was some pretty heavy stuff that you laid out for them, but I think they're old enough to understand."

"I feel like I got my children back." Melissa smiled. "For so long, I've felt like I was alone, and we were so torn apart that we wouldn't be able to get back together again."

"Like Humpty Dumpty?" Aunt Elaine joked.

Melissa swallowed the lump that had formed in her throat again. "Exactly like that."

Aunt Elaine patted her on the shoulder. "I'm glad you were wrong."

"Me too." Melissa grinned.

"Now," Aunt Elaine said and chin-pointed to the living room. "Don't forget you have a guest. It was a good idea calling him."

"Gemma's idea," Melissa admitted.

"I always knew she was a smart girl." Aunt Elaine winked as she walked off to join the kids in the living room.

Melissa's heart swelled with pride as she walked behind Aunt Elaine, and when Ian turned to look at her, her heart melted in a different way.

Chapter Twenty-Four

Ian got up when he saw her.

Gemma and Max were still fighting over which movie to watch, and Ian walked around them on his way to her. She led him back to the kitchen so they could talk before he left.

"I can't thank you enough for leaving whatever you were doing to come down here and help me to find Max. I appreciate it more than you know."

"Uh, I have a pretty good idea of how much." He smiled at her, his eyes twinkling and his face glowing in a way she'd never seen before. Or had refused to see before.

She laughed. "Always the modest one."

He chuckled too. "I can't help it."

He heaved an exasperated sigh and walked around to the other side of the table. His face had suddenly gotten very serious, and when he looked back at her, she could see the pain in his eyes. She was confused by it, and she inched closer.

"What's wrong?"

He smiled wryly, not answering at first, and just toyed with the coasters on the table. She could tell his mind had drifted off to a place where he was hurt.

"Maybe you should sit," he said to her and pulled out a chair.

"Uh-oh," she replied and slowly sat. "This can't be good."

He chuckled. 'It's not that bad. I just wanted to share something with you that I never have, and I think now is an appropriate time to do it."

"Okay," she said as she started to imagine what he could have to tell her that was so important.

"Remember how I told you that I used to live in the city and then I moved here?"

"Yes," Melissa said as she remembered their conversation from the park. "You were Mr. Wall Street gone country."

He smiled. "Yeah, you could say that. What I didn't tell you was the other reason why I left the big city."

"Go on," Melissa said as she leaned forward and perched on the edge of her chair.

"I was married," he said.

And her heart stopped. She wasn't sure why she was so shocked by it, but the revelation left her speechless, nonetheless. "Okay," she drawled.

"I loved her. Would do anything for her. In fact, I did," he said as a wave of nostalgia swept over him. "I worked myself to the bone to provide the kind of life she wanted. She liked nice things, and I made sure she had them. I went out of my way to make sure she was happy and comfortable," he said as he sighed and wiped his hand down his face. "We never had children, and she wanted them," he continued. "So did I. We tried for a really long time, and nothing."

"I'm so sorry," Melissa said as sadness came over her like a wet blanket. She couldn't imagine how devastating that was to want something so badly and be denied repeatedly.

"Yeah," he said and toyed with the coaster. "Sometimes I wonder if it wasn't a good thing in the long run—that she and I never had kids. But anyway, when she couldn't get pregnant, she blamed me."

Melissa narrowed her eyes. "Why you? It could be either of you. Or both. Or none."

"I know that, but maybe it was the stress at the time, and she didn't want to blame herself, so she blamed me."

"How?" Melissa asked.

"She said I worked too hard," he continued with a sigh and sat back against the chair. "The same job I was working to make sure she was okay turned into the monster and me with it."

"What did you do?" Melissa was curious to know.

"I worked for a retail chain, so I traveled a lot, which meant I didn't spend as much time at home. I couldn't. When I used to, she'd complain about bills and food and vacation being postponed because there wasn't enough money. When I got another job that paid enough and then some, it was still a problem. I started to realize that I couldn't please her."

"Didn't she realize that you wouldn't be having a child either?" Melissa asked sympathetically. So many times, society forgot that men had feelings, too, and that they experienced the same losses women were celebrated as strong for overcoming.

"I guess not," he groaned. "But because of her being

so unhappy and my guilt, I ended up switching careers just so I could please her. But that wasn't enough either. She wanted to live a flashy life, and with less money, that started to become an issue again. We were back at square one, and I was at my wit's end. We started spending less and less time together until she quit on me altogether." Ian's eyes grew glossy from the memory, and his lips tightened. "I was a broken man after that. Not only did she send me divorce papers, but she also took my dreams of ever having a family again."

A new lump formed in Melissa's throat. "I'm so sorry you had to go through that. I had no idea. No wonder you came here and want to stay away from people."

He smiled. "Yep. Now I just stick to the predictability of land and a tree lot. That is until some kid comes up to me and asks me to decorate the whole lot to cheer up their mother, and then that's the highlight of my year."

Melissa laughed. "How did you know about Yuletide Creek?"

"I've been here before, and it's also on the other side of the map," he told her. "No chance of running into anyone I knew. I needed a fresh start and here seemed the perfect place. I had some money saved up, so I was able to get the lot and do my own thing on my own terms."

"Good for you." Melissa smiled. "I'm just trying to pick myself up by the bootstraps as well. Relationships are complicated, aren't they?"

"Uh, I wouldn't say that off the bat," he said and shook his head from side to side. "It's really good when you're with the right person or someone who sees you for you or appreciates you."

Melissa blushed. "You're right, but my standards are very low. I don't have much to compare with. I was married to Peter for over twenty years, and now I find myself in unfamiliar territory."

"So, basically, we're two lonely people who don't have a clue how to navigate these waters?" he asked and chuckled.

"Yes!" Melissa replied emphatically.

"The thing is," Ian said and leaned forward, "I thought I was fine, you know? I had a business. I had some money. I was alone without fearing the harsh admonitions of a fiery tongue. I thought I was doing great. And then I met you."

Melissa's eyes popped, and she tapped her chest. "Me? What did I do?"

"I knew there was something different about you from the first day I saw you on the side of the road looking clueless."

Melissa laughed. "You must be joking? Are we talking about the same day when I was so rude to you and refused your help out of pride?"

He snickered. "The very same."

Melissa blushed and covered her face. "I don't know how you were nice to me after that." She stared at the table for a while, and when she looked up, he was looking intensely at her. "What?"

"Do you really want to know why?" he asked and leaned forward. She nodded. "I saw something in you that I recognized. I knew you were a broken woman trying to do right and not depend on anyone ever again. That's what I saw, and that's why I never held it against you. I understood. I was the same way for a long time. After a marriage like we had, how could we not want to live life on our own terms with no one standing over our shoulders questioning everything we're doing?"

"I know what you mean, but really? You saw all that?"

"Hey, you had no clue how to change that tire, and you didn't want me to help. That speaks volumes."

Melissa's earlier blush deepened. "I must have looked like such an idiot."

"No." He smiled. "I liked the goodies it landed me."

She laughed. "Well, I'm glad you weren't mad at me."

"You want to know something else?" he asked. "You know how badly I've wanted a family and how I gave up on that dream?"

"Yeah." She nodded.

"This might sound a little crazy, but every time I'm with you and the kids, although they're not really kids anymore, I feel like I'm with my family. It feels so natural."

Melissa's heart swelled. "I can tell. I saw the way you were with Max in the woods. You're a natural father, so no, it's not crazy at all. In fact, it's one of the things I love most about you."

"Really?" he asked and attempted to bat his eyes in jest. "Tell me more."

Melissa erupted into laughter before she covered her mouth so she wouldn't attract anyone to their conversation. "You're crazy, you know that?"

"Maybe," he replied and leaned back again.

It was Melissa's time to get somber as she started thinking about her own journey. "After Peter, I was sure that I'd never be with anyone ever again. I mean, how could I? I'm past my prime, and what man would want a broken woman with two grown kids? But then you came along, and even though we're not really an item or anything, you filled the void he left. Look at what you did tonight. I couldn't have gotten through to Max. He responds better to male authority figures in the same way his father would get things done that I couldn't."

"He's a boy, and so were we," Ian interjected. "We understand some of what he's feeling and experiencing because we've been there."

"I still think it's more than that." She smiled. "I just want to say how much I appreciate you."

"It goes both ways." He grinned.

She was silent for a couple of seconds before she spoke again. "Would you think I'm crazy if I tell you that I'm thinking of staying in Yuletide Creek?"

His face lit up like a Christmas tree. "I like that kind of crazy. Of course, I like that idea! Took you long enough."

She laughed. "I've been playing with the idea."

"But I don't know how that's going to work out for us. I'm not so sure I'm cut out for the hustle and bustle of the city life in town," he joked.

Melissa giggled. "I'm sure you'll figure it out."

"I guess I'll have to." He smirked.

"Mom!" Max said as he slid into view. "We found a movie."

"I guess that's my cue," Ian said and stood.

"Sorry, but duty calls," she said as she walked him to the door. "Thanks again for coming over."

"It's not like I was doing anything all by myself up in the mountains." He grinned and shoved his hands into his pockets and rocked on his heels.

"How about coming over for dinner tomorrow?" she asked him. "We have plenty, and no one should be alone on Christmas, let alone you."

"I'd love that." He smiled. "See you tomorrow?"

"Yep." Melissa grinned.

She stood by the door and watched as he got into his truck and drove off. The butterflies in her stomach started acting up, and she clutched her chest and turned, only to witness Max shaking his head at her.

"Ready?" he asked her.

"I'm coming! Sheesh!" she said as she hurried into the living room and cozied up with the throw. "What are we watching?"

"*Home Alone* 2!" Gemma replied. "It was literally the only thing we could agree on."

"She's not lying." Aunt Elaine laughed. "They are like polar opposites, these two. Or they try to be."

"I think it's the latter," Melissa said. "Okay. Showtime!"

Max dimmed the lights as the family cuddled on the sofa with gingerbread cookies on their lap. It was the most normal Christmas Melissa had seen in years.

Chapter Twenty-Five

"Wake up, everybody! It's Christmas!" Max shouted the following morning.

"Oh my goodness," Melissa groaned and yawned. "It's like waking up on the Home Alone set."

Max laughed. "Just get up, Mom. I want to open my presents."

"You make it sound as if you have a ton," she said and rolled out of bed. "At least let me wash up first."

Melissa met Gemma in the bathroom, her hair just as crumpled and matted as Melissa's, with the sleep still hanging on their eyelids.

"You asked for it," Gemma said to her of Max. "He's back, and it's like he's eight all over again."

"Yeah," Melissa agreed. "What time is it?"

"Let's just say it's an ungodly hour for anyone to be awake," Gemma said.

The two women stood in front of the mirror, brushing their teeth in unison before they separated to their rooms. Melissa felt like a zombie as she slipped into her sweatpants and matching top before she remembered the onesie they should be wearing.

She dashed over to Gemma's room. "You're wearing this, right?"

Gemma was already wearing it. "Apparently," she sulked. "Although I could go for what you're wearing now."

"No, I forgot for a minute. I'll change them, and I hope Max knows I have one for him too," Melissa said with a wide smile. "That will be my revenge."

Max was sitting in the living room staring at the tree when Melissa crept up behind him. He turned and narrowed his eyes. "No!" he said right away when he saw the outfit in her hands.

"Max, we're dressing alike this Christmas, so come on, or it's no presents for you," Melissa warned.

"Do I really have to?" he asked as his shoulders sagged. "What's wrong with ordinary pajamas?"

"Hey, suck it up! If I have to wear one, so do you," Gemma said as she came down the stairs.

One look at her and Max burst into laughter. "Mom, I cannot look like that today," Max pleaded.

"It's not so bad," Aunt Elaine said as she appeared, wearing the red Santa Claus-themed onesie. "It's actually quite comfortable."

"It looks silly," Max replied.

"Okay, you don't have to wear it," Melissa said to him and tossed the onesie onto the sofa.

"What? How come he doesn't get to wear it, and I do?" Gemma asked in dismay. "I look like Rudolph barfed on me."

Max giggled. "Luck of the draw."

"I wouldn't say that," Melissa said to Max. "You don't get to open any presents otherwise, so pick your poison."

"Ha!" Gemma laughed and pointed at him as she mocked him. "Have that!"

Max's face fell, and then he got up and grabbed the onesie from the sofa as if it was the thing's fault. His face was mopping the floor when he came back downstairs.

Gemma started snickering.

"Gemma, be nice. You don't look any different," Melissa told her.

"Do I have to wear this *all* day?" Max lamented. "I feel like an idiot."

"You look nice, my little reindeer," Melissa said and pinched his cheeks.

"Not helping," Max told her.

Everyone started laughing as Max repositioned himself in front of the tree.

"Okay, gather around everyone," Melissa said as she ushered them closer. "We all know this year has been a trying one. Well, the last couple of years, to say the least. I know that we've all had our rough times, but we've also had good times. This Christmas is one of those good times. We're blessed to be here in Yuletide Creek with Aunt Elaine, who was so gracious to share her home with us."

"Uh, Mom, can we save the speech until after?" Max asked.

Gemma snickered. "On that, we agree."

"I'm saying some important stuff here," Melissa argued.

"Say it over breakfast," Aunt Elaine said as she moved toward the tree. "We've waited long enough. I want to see what I got."

And everyone took that as their cue. They raced to the tree, and boxes started flying as they were passed to their respective owners. Paper ripped from the boxes and made a carpet on the floor as they all dove in.

"Neat," Max said when he saw the gift card. "Who's this from?"

"Oh, Grandma Johnson wasn't sure what you wanted, so she figured she'd send the money instead," Melissa answered.

"Cool." Max grinned.

Gemma loved the shiny new earrings that Melissa got for her, her gift card, and the boots and scarf Aunt Elaine bought.

Max was just as over the moon when he saw the pair of Jordans he'd always wanted, courtesy of Betty and Dick.

Melissa got a gift card as well as some shiny trinkets and a framed family photo. Aunt Elaine couldn't complain either. She got something from everyone.

"I don't care what was in these gift bags. I got my Christmas gift when you all came here for the holidays," she said as tears formed in her eyes. "This may be my best Christmas yet."

"Aww," Gemma and Melissa gushed as they rushed over to hug her.

"We love being here," Melissa said. "In fact, that's my other surprise. How would you two like to stay here? And by you two, I mean Max since Gemma may be flying off to the other side of the world," Melissa said and rolled her eyes.

"Dramatic much?" Gemma laughed.

"I don't mind," Max replied.

"Then it's settled. Aunt Elaine, we're officially here to stay."

The woman threw herself into Melissa's arms as tears ran down her face. "Merry Christmas!"

"Merry Christmas, everybody!" Max said as he hopped over the back of the sofa. "Now, let's eat!"

"Oh no, you don't!" Melissa called after him. "Please pick up these wrappers before you leave here."

"I'll go and heat up the roast beef," Aunt Elaine said as Max returned to help with the cleaning.

In another couple of minutes, they were all sitting at the breakfast table with a spread of toast, egg and potato casserole, bacon, pumpkin cinnamon rolls, and ginger-bread muffins. There was also spiced coffee and hot chocolate, and everyone had a healthy serving.

"I'm going to call Grandma Betty," Melissa said as she stuffed a piece of muffin into her mouth. Aunt Elaine looked a little anxious, but she came around as soon as Betty and Dick came onto the screen.

"Merry Christmas!" they all shouted, and Max and Gemma hooted.

"Merry Christmas!" Betty replied.

"Dad, you're finally around." Melissa laughed. "Every time I call, you're out doing something or the other."

"You can't blame me." He chuckled. "How are you doing, Elaine?"

"I'm doing great now that I've stolen your daughter and her kids," Aunt Elaine joked, and Dick hooted uproariously.

"It's good to hear from you and see you," he said. "You look well."

"Thank you," Aunt Elaine replied with a smile and a blush.

"Thanks for the gift, Grandma," Gemma shouted.

"You're welcome, baby," Betty replied.

"I don't know if Mom told you, but I'm thinking of coming to that side of the world soon," Gemma said excitedly and watched as her grandmother's face started shining with happiness.

"Really? I didn't know about that," Betty remarked.

"That's because I haven't come to terms with it yet," Melissa said. "I can't imagine her so far away from home."

"She'll be fine," Betty replied and waved her off.

"I guess you don't get all the children Elaine." Dick laughed.

Aunt Elaine laughed too. "I guess not."

"Hey, that breakfast looks good," Betty said after a while. "I did always love your cooking, Elaine."

"I made some of them," Melissa interjected. "I did the bacon and coffee."

Betty snickered. "I guess you can call that help."

"You're mean," Melissa replied, much to Gemma's amusement.

The lively banter continued right through breakfast. Everyone was in a good mood as they tidied the kitchen and packed away the breakfast plates.

"Can you believe it's already past noon?" Aunt Elaine exclaimed when her eyes caught the clock. "We're going to have to go right into dinner preparations."

"Ugh!" Melissa groaned. "I love Christmas, but I hate all the work it comes with. I am not looking forward to taking down all of these decorations either."

Aunt Elaine chuckled. "Why do you think I never bother to put them up? There's plenty to see in town. If I want to see lights, I can go to Christmas Town."

Melissa laughed. "I'm beginning to see the wisdom in that."

Max and Gemma disappeared while Melissa and Aunt Elaine remained in the kitchen. Melissa dressed the table, and the dishes were heated. Aunt Elaine made the garden salad, and by three, everything was done. The house smelled like heaven as the delicious blend of aromas filled the air.

"I smell food," Max said as he bounded downstairs, still wearing his onesie.

"Hey, I thought you would have changed out of this," Melissa observed.

"It is actually pretty warm," he said with a wide grin.

"Told ya." Aunt Elaine giggled.

"Is it dinner time?" Max asked as he headed for the dining room.

"Not yet. We're expecting company, and I will not be seen in this, so excuse me," Melissa said and hurried upstairs. Her heart raced for the entire time it took her to get dressed. She couldn't stop thinking about him and the way he made her feel. He'd turned an otherwise disastrous Christmas into a happy memory for her and sharing their first Christmas dinner was like the cherry on top of her sundae.

She slipped into a sweater dress that revealed her full figure, fluffed her hair, and added light makeup before she returned downstairs. She'd barely stepped onto the landing when she spotted Ian, and her heart did a somersault.

"Ian, when did you get here?" she asked as her cheeks began to warm.

"Just now," he said as his eyes swept over her. "Wow," he mouthed.

"Thanks," she said as she observed his casual jeans and red button-down. As simple as it looked, he made it sexier. "You don't look so bad yourself."

"If you'd told me this was a dress-up party, I'd have gotten a onesie too," he joked.

Melissa laughed. "I'd love to have seen that."

"Maybe you will next year," he said, hinting at future Christmases together. It was something to look forward to.

"Okay, are we all here?" Aunt Elaine asked.

"Yep," Melissa replied.

"Then, let's dig in," she said and called them over.

"I can carve that turkey if you need a hand," Ian offered. "I'm a professional carver."

Gemma snickered. "Is that a thing?"

"Everything's a thing." Ian grinned. "You just have to make it so. Next thing you know, everyone will be calling me to carve their turkeys."

Max chuckled. "Not a very marketable skill. You'd only have a job two months of the year."

Ian nodded in agreement. "You have a point, but that wasn't mine. You can be great at anything," he said as he used the knife to point at both her and Gemma, who received his advice with a smile. "Okay, enough with the talking. I'll do my thing."

And he wasn't lying. They had never seen cleaner cuts of turkey, and after they complimented him, Ian placed the knife to his lips and blew on it as if it was a smoking gun. "Told ya!"

Everyone started laughing as they passed various plates of collard greens, beans, and salad across the table.

Melissa was glowing as she watched her family and realized how happy everyone was. Ian seemed right at home with them. She remembered everything she'd gone through, and she couldn't help the feeling that it was going to be one of her favorite Christmases.

The kids were in far better spirits, and even though it wasn't postcard-perfect, she couldn't imagine it being any better.

Other Books by Kimberly

An Oak Harbor Series

The Archer Inn

A Yuletide Creek Series

Connect with Kimberly Thomas

Facebook
Newsletter
BookBub
Amazon

Made in United States
North Haven, CT
21 October 2023

43031236R00113